as we continue to reimagine the world according to Allende's legacy...Dorfman is a global writer at a time when we need his magnitude of understanding, as well as his gentle loyalty to roots, the Earth, and memory, which together have sustained the author's lifelong belief in human beings and justice."
—*Markaz Review*

"A unique and uniquely gripping book, a mix of memoir and fiction of a sort I've never seen before."
—Tom Engelhardt,
SouthernCross Review

"*The Suicide Museum* is a memoir, a mystery, a tragedy, a philosophical treatise, a song of homecoming, and a spectacular mix of the real and the imagined. In this novel Ariel Dorfman puts his whole literary life on the page—and what a life it has been! For decades Dorfman has written in defiance of the ordinary. He gets to the very pulse of who we are: the social, the political, the artistic, and beyond. Right down to its moment of last-line grace, *The Suicide Museum* keeps the essential questions alive and, at the same time, joins us all together."
—Colum McCann, National Book Award–winning
author of *Let the Great World Spin*

"A master storyteller uses the devices of fiction to shine a light on the mysteries of real life—and to push ever deeper into everything that haunts him: what a culminating gift from an essential spokesman for humanity and conscience."
—Pico Iyer, national bestselling author of
The Half Known Life

"Ariel Dorfman has created a history book disguised as a mystery, or maybe a mystery written as history. Lodged between memoir and fiction, *The Suicide Museum* is a labyrinth of mirrors, a tale of one nation, or perhaps all nations, where the tortured are condemned to live alongside their torturers. An intricate, thought-provoking read by a literary magician."

—Sandra Cisneros, national bestselling author of *The House on Mango Street*

"The wildly brilliant Ariel Dorfman has outdone himself with this rivetingly original and mesmerizingly profound supernova of a novel… *The Suicide Museum* is so many perfect things: a globetrotting mystery, a courageous journey into Chile's nightmare past, a tender paean to the bonds that keep us human, but above all it's just about the best book I've read in a decade."

—Junot Díaz, author of the Pulitzer Prize and National Book Critics Circle Award–winning novel *The Brief Wondrous Life of Oscar Wao*

"At the crossroads of history and memory, the masterful Ariel Dorfman has given us a portrait of a generation that lived under the shadow of Fidel Castro and Che, and then suffered the destruction of the alternate vision of socialism offered by Salvador Allende—a tragedy that haunts us still."

—Alma Guillermoprieto, author of *Dancing with Cuba: A Memoir of the Revolution*

"In this engrossing novel, Ariel Dorfman has found the perfect sweet spot where history, politics, and literary fiction blend. Dorfman, like some of his major characters, operates as an archeologist digging into the remains of recent traumas. Anyone interested in how the past impinges on the present and is transformed into art, should read this book."

—Ian Buruma, author of *The Collaborators: Three Stories of Deception and Survival in World War II*

"Ariel Dorfman is surely the modern-day conscience of Latin America. He is the elegant scribe of its blue sky as well as its iron fist. He is the clear-eyed, loyal witness to its sputtering bids for democracy. *The Suicide Museum* is the story he was always meant to write. In it, his prodigious talents are everywhere in evidence—in his breathtaking gifts as a storyteller; in his fierce pursuit of history's truths; in his sly, deliciously wicked humor; in his essential humanity. This is a riveting novel with a large brain, big heart, and a dark secret at its core. It deserves a universe of readers."

—Marie Arana, prize-winning author of *American Chica, Bolívar: American Liberator,* and *Silver, Sword, and Stone*

"I was enthralled by Ariel Dorfman's *The Suicide Museum.* I have always loved his writing, loved performing his poetry *Last Waltz in Santiago,* but this work twisted my heart. To be the expat, the outsider without a home, looking for a way back in is so powerful and lonely. His scrupulous search for the truth holds us all to a very high standard."

—Kathleen Turner, Golden Globe Award–winning actress

"A novel that is also an elegy that in its mournful and nostalgic funeral song exalts the figure of Allende as a moral hero of a generation... This is a novel of multiple paths that intersect and interweave, and where the reader goes up and down different floors, entering and leaving the various levels of reality as they open, a history of the homeland, autobiography, testimony, chronicle, journalistic story, detective story, all of which, seen as a whole, is what a novel should best be according to Cervantes. *The Suicide Museum* is total and totalizing, an imaginative artifact to understand the occurrences of history and learn to read reality through fiction."

—Sergio Ramírez, author of
Divine Punishment

"*The Suicide Museum* is a thrilling crossroads of genres, where history, chronicle, autofiction, memoir, thriller, and essay converge, and where a complex moral reflection and a call to political rebellion take the form of an investigation into one of the fundamental myths of the twentieth century: the death of Salvador Allende. Ariel Dorfman has written the book of his life."

—Javier Cercas, author of
Soldiers of Salamis and *The Impostor*

"A hallucinatory novel that opens up multiple questions and whose central theme is ultimately the impossibility of language to access death."

—Raúl Zurita, Cervantes Prize winner and
author of *Sky Below: Selected Works*

"*The Suicide Museum* reminds us why we need fiction to understand the traumas of our Latin American history. Dorfman has written a daring and lucid novel, which makes for compulsive reading and has great formal wisdom."

—Juan Gabriel Vásquez, author of
The Sound of Things Falling and *The Shape of the Ruins*

"The author of *Death and the Maiden* has done it again: this novel transforms the dark memory of Chile into a meditation on history, guilt, and the traces left by horror. To read this is indispensable on the fiftieth anniversary of Pinochet's coup d'état." —Santiago Roncagliolo, author of *Red April*

"What a formidable artifact...something like a cross between Norman Mailer, Don DeLillo, and—last but not least and before anyone else and above all—Ariel Dorfman."

—Rodrigo Fresán, author of *Kensington Gardens*

"Highly recommended...An impressive mix of novel and essay...It will have many readers and deserves a warm reception."

—Benjamín Prado, author of
Not Only Fire and *Snow Is Silent*

ALLEGRO

ALSO BY ARIEL DORFMAN

ALLEGRO

Ariel Dorfman

Other Press
New York

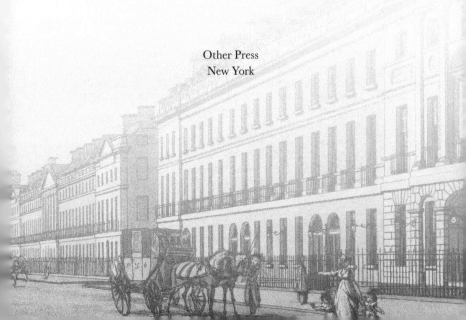

Title-page image: *Portland Place*, etching and aquatint by
Thomas Malton the younger, 1800, Royal Academy of Arts, London

Production editor: Yvonne E. Cárdenas
Text designer: Patrice Sheridan
This book was set in Baskervelle MT and Aire Bold Pro
by Alpha Design & Composition of Pittsfield, NH

1 3 5 7 9 10 8 6 4 2

Library of Congress Cataloging-in-Publication Data
Names: Dorfman, Ariel, author.
Title: Allegro / Ariel Dorfman.
Other titles: Allegro. English
Description: New York : Other Press, 2025. | "A version of this novel was
originally published in Spanish as Allegro in 2015 by Editorial
Stella Maris, Barcelona."—Title page verso.
Identifiers: LCCN 2024026102 (print) | LCCN 2024026103 (ebook) |
ISBN 9781635424485 (paperback) | ISBN 9781635424492 (ebook)
Subjects: LCSH: Mozart, Wolfgang Amadeus, 1756-1791—Fiction. |
Bach, Johann Sebastian, 1685-1750—Death and burial—Fiction. | Handel,
George Frideric, 1685-1759—Death and burial—Fiction. | LCGFT:
Biographical fiction. | Detective and mystery fiction. | Novels.
Classification: LCC PQ8098.14.O7 A64413 2025 (print) |
LCC PQ8098.14.O7 (ebook) | DDC 863/.64—dc23/eng/20241016
LC record available at https://lccn.loc.gov/2024026102
LC ebook record available at https://lccn.loc.gov/2024026103

Publisher's Note
This is a work of fiction. Names, characters, places, and incidents either are the
product of the author's imagination or are used fictitiously.

For Angélica, music of my life.

And for Eric, our light, our life, our song.

AUTHOR'S NOTE: In *Allegro* all musical offerings, dates, characters, and public events, with some minor exceptions, are factually true. Their existence may be consulted in the historical record. Everything else in this divertimento is an invention, a two- and three- and four-part invention, with many a voice intervening.

For those readers interested in accompanying their experience of *Allegro* with the music that inspired the author as he wrote and that accompanied the characters as they lived their real and fictional lives, there is a Playlist at the end of this book registering the pertinent compositions, arranged in the order in which they appear over the course of the novel.

Leipzig, April 22, 1789

Overture

I came to Leipzig, lost, in search of a sign.

What did I hope to find? Some manner of guidance from a dead composer? A message left behind among the living? Or some other sort of contact floating in the air, awaiting someone adrift like me, someone who had not even been born when that musician expired, not far from where I now stand, in this very city?

So absurd and desperate a quest could not be communicated to those who care for me, least of all to Constanze, who would have seen it as more evidence that I was unhinged, harrowed by debt, and sliding into melancholia. King Frederick requires me in Potsdam, I told her, he will award me a post that will solve all our problems.

Though nothing of the kind was true. As Leipzig was on the route to Potsdam, she would not find it entirely strange that I should stop here, offer a concert, replenish my coffers for a while, bring her back a pittance. Impossible to tell my loving little wife that I expected a whisper from God or somebody else to visit me.

One last chance before I must depart. For the third time in three days, I stand again in front of the grave next to St. John's Church where Johann Sebastian Bach lies—six paces from the south corner of the building. It was almost forty years ago that he last saw the light, saw the light and lost it, was twice blinded, and then, and then ... What happened then?

Of all those who know the answer, of the three men who may have known it, none is alive today. Only I remain, only I have an inkling as to whether it was a crime or an act of absolution that night, what door was opened—or did it close forever?—in the room where the great composer took holy Communion as he lay dying, only I can bear witness, trying to puzzle out the truth, separate falsehood from its illusions, only this ailing man of thirty-four who stares at that unspeaking grave, myself calling out to the man who brought me here.

The friend I will never see again.

Part One

LONDON

~

FIRST CHAPTER

London, February 2, 1765

Allegro Ma Non Troppo

The man approached me barely a few seconds after the concert had ended, before the applause had died down. And yet his voice had a piercing, flutelike quality that carried above the clapping and the murmurs and the chatter—and indeed he was thin as a reed himself, and rather ungainly, but not unpleasant, an agreeable voice that might sing well if given the festive occasion. And he must have had many such occasions, because his forty-some years had clearly seen cheerful times, as a sparkle in his eye attested and his sumptuous attire confirmed, no matter how miserable an expression he now wore. But that was not what really called my attention.

"A word with you, young master," he said, in a manner most bold.

He was addressing me in my native German tongue—
everything correct and grammatical and in its orderly place,
laden though the words were with the nasal, stilted accents
of English vowels. Not dense enough to put me off, at any
rate—I was such a child at the time, my ninth birthday celebrated a mere week earlier, and homesick to the bones. *You
will get used to it*, my father had insisted, *you cannot aspire to the
sort of life you deserve, that the family deserves, if you and your sister
do not travel widely, if you do not seek your fortunes beyond Salzburg.* There were few people in London who talked to me
in German, and my English was worse than rudimentary,
despite my ability to imitate every sound I had ever heard—
my French and Italian were already perfect! So even if he
had not sported a forlorn and abandoned air, I would have
listened gladly to the man who called me "young master,"
and more so as he was filling my ears with flattering words
about the symphony that had just now been exposed to a select audience in Carlisle House but soon would be admired
by connoisseurs in the wide world who had not been privileged to attend the premiere of my princely recital, far better
what you have composed, he assured me, than the offerings
of Johann Christian Bach or Carl Friedrich Abel, that had
preceded and followed my own divine harmony, that's what
he called it.

Though a mere whip of a boy, I had fallen into the habit
of lapping up such accolades, all those adjectives, *divine, majestic, invincible, all-powerful*, which my own Papa frequently
echoed, joining the river of praise that coiled around me,

more, more, every superlative had been poured on my head
like an endless baptismal fount and I desired more, I wanted
that river to spill into an endless sea. And yet, and yet, the
man was overreaching, he was magnifying my attributes
beyond what even my own parents extolled, he may have
meant every word but that was not the reason for his adu-
lation. It must have been the way he smacked his lips as if
he had just tasted the most delicious sauce, the way he let a
smile break out as he genuflected. The uneven teeth inside
his mouth did not dispel my sympathy for him. It was so
guileless, that smile, like that of a little boy who has received
the blessing of a father rather than a beating upon returning
home full of sweat and mud. So full of hope.

He wanted something from me.

Alerted by his excess, I should perhaps have refused
him, not engaged a total stranger.

Though he wasn't entirely a stranger.

I had remarked his lanky, elegant presence already at
several junctures over the past few months, at concerts offered by other musicians and at the King's Theatre during
the performances of the opera *Adriano in Siria* and the pasticcio *Ezio*, as well as at paid presentations when I myself had
appeared publicly with my sister Nannerl to an explosion of
acclaim, the man had been there, hovering on the outskirts
of my attention. Gawking at me hungrily, never attempting
to draw near, with a haunted aura, his eyes darting from
me to my father, to my sister, to my mother on the rare occasions when she happened to be present, inspecting them

with a gaze that was decidedly not like the one he directed at my person, as if I were a castle and they the moat, I the treasure and they the dragons.

Tonight was different—for him and for me.

Tonight he had brought along a skinny lad, close to my own age, the first thing I realized when I glimpsed him loitering in the audience, at the back of Mrs. Teresa Cornelys's grandiose, brocaded hall. He's brought his son tonight, I thought, must be some relative. Why, the boy brandishes a similar glum look that is just as evidently artificial.

Pathetic.

Even before I heard the man's voice, I recognized a certain cajoling, scraping worship of power, even before he had bowed with far too much abasement as he called me "young master" in German, I recognized how he had lived, how he had survived, how someone had taught him that we cannot advance in the world unless potentates are satisfied, those who hold the purse strings and those who bestow honors and those who can kick you in the ass or lift you in their arms to glory, we cannot press forward in life unless we learn to lower our eyes and buckle our knees and insist that we are their most obedient and humble servants. A lesson my father had drilled into me. But not the only one. *Because inside, Woferl,* my father always insisted, *inside you are free to think as you will, inside you know that you have what they do not, that God has given you inordinately more than He will ever give them. And let that certainty provide sustenance for the difficult years that are sure to greet you once you grow up and are no longer a child prodigy, once you must, as I have been forced to do, earn your bread as a musician in a merciless world.*

Did that thin man now in front of me know that about himself? Had his own father taught him to keep some sense of self-worth in reserve? Or was he so famished for whatever favor I could offer that he had forgotten all dignity?

As if he could hear my inner musings, he ceased his compliments, and in a voice so squat that only he and I could harken to it, he scooted a question at me: "Can you keep a secret, Master Mozart?"

Intrigued by this unforeseen turn of events, I did not hesitate to answer in the affirmative, of course I could keep a secret.

"And are you ready, dear sir, to gallop to the rescue of an old man who has been much maligned and abused and has need of redress, can you help restore his honor?"

I nodded. It was like a fairy tale, how could I not give my assent?

"You must swear that you will tell no one of this conversation," the man continued. "Save for one man, save for the London Bach, Johann Christian Bach, son of the incomparable Johann Sebastian, deceased these fifteen years," and his eyes scurried in the direction of the Kapellmeister, still standing close to the podium receiving congratulations for his own newest Sinfonia Concertante, written exclusively for this subscription series. "If you were willing to accomplish this epic task, I would be evermore in your debt, as would the older man to whom I have made reference. Will you, shall you, can you, do this, young sir?"

His need was so blatant and urgent that it appealed to my kindness, how else to respond except with the affection and amiability that stemmed so naturally from my spirit, and I was about to say yes, yes, of course, dear sir, when I was struck by a chilling thought: What if he were a spy? An actor hired by my father to test me? *Trust no one, Wolfgang, especially doctors,* was one of his cantilenas, an eternal ritornello. Perhaps my beloved Papa had decided to use some third-rate acquaintance of Garrick's to see if, on the first night I was away from his benevolent eye, I succumbed to the dreaded belief in the goodness of all people. Was this man's countenance not too perfect? Had my parents—but, no, my mother would not be part of such a scheme, she would never deceive me, even for my own gain—had my father trained him, coaxed from the fellow the sort of woebegone demeanor that would reach my heart and make it melt with compassion? Directed him as if he were a town fiddler, a piper of the lowest sort? But not the lowest, no, rather a consummate professional: if this was a mask, like those I loved to parade at Carnival, it was fleshed onto his face like a second skin. No, my father could not have afforded someone of that high caliber, would not have wasted the few guineas that we barely called our own merely to test me—and anyway Papa could never have forecast that I would be left alone tonight or any other night or day or afternoon or morning or noontime without his vigilance, without his advice as to whom I should mistrust.

For once, and the first time in my life, whether I trusted this thin man or not depended entirely on my solitary judgment, not to be determined by fear of my father's anger or yearning for his approval. It was a test, but one devised not by Leopold Mozart but by God himself, an initial lesson in how to read underneath the pleasant surface mendacity of each admirer, God teaching me to curb my outgoing personality and the automatic—and therefore far too easy— pity I feel, like a silly sponge, for any needy soul who staggers across my path, God preparing me for the day when, alone in the world, I would have to discern for myself who was my enemy and who my friend.

So what to do, if mercifulness was not a reliable road to tread? Was there something else in this cautionary case, some other desire that could guide me? There was. The intruder had asked if I could keep a secret, he had implied there was a mission he wished to charge me with, an adventure. That was the reason I should say yes, because I was as eager for an escapade—oh, admit it, Wolfgang—as he was for the service I might provide him.

That he was accosting me on this night of all nights surely should induce me to be open to his advances.

It was a miracle that I was even there, unescorted as never before, free of loving eyes and beloved guardian fingers and adult bodies shielding me from hostile or benign incursions. A miracle that I had feared and awaited in equal measure. A miracle that this man had obviously been awaiting as well for months, though possessed of a fear very distinct from mine: that an opportunity to approach me unmolested would never materialize.

It had almost not arrived at all.

I had awoken that very Saturday morning earlier than usual. With one bound I was out of bed, jerked upright and in motion before my eyes draped themselves open, tremulous with excitement.

Today was the day! Today I would hear Maestro Bach present my symphony, the inaugural offering of so many—I could already envisage a long stretch of similar works ahead of me, I was already finishing the second and the third, would start next week on the fourth symphony—today was the day, tonight the night. Oh, *molto allegro* my outlook, like the first movement of my first symphony, very joyful and buoyant, all the people who would come up to me and tell me how much they loved me and my work, all the pretty ladies and their kisses, today, today.

But wait, it was deathly quiet outside 21 Thrift Street, a shimmer of ghostly light was swirling out there in Soho, ominously drifting behind the drawn curtains. I stumbled to the window, stubbing my toe against the clavichord Papa had rented, I stifled the hint of a cry that surged to my lips. I did not wish to wake the household yet, not yet, I wanted a few more minutes alone.

A mere slit in the curtains so I could peer out.

My heart sank.

It was snowing, coming down hard. Wondrously beautiful, I would have cried out in Salzburg on a magical morn when we would go, the whole family and a horde of friends, for a sleigh ride, I would have called each flake a slight letter from God. But not here, in London. Here the message from heaven was the opposite: it implied that the streets might be malignant, icicles were hanging on the gates of our transitory home like secretions, saliva, the hard dribble from a dead man's mouth. And the message from inside the bowels of our residence confirmed the bad news: the first sound of the day was my father retching, vomiting in a way that reminded me of how his stomach had turned inside out on the crossing from Calais to Dover. All the other passengers were astonished that one individual could generate such a barrel of half-digested fare, there were six of them, wide-eyed and swaying, besides us, taken on by Herr Leopold Mozart to alleviate the objectionable cost of the transportation—well, this bout of heaving rivaled that one.

And then a second sound. My dear sister's cough, worse than yesterday's, hoarse and persistent and spiteful.

And finally a third sound. My mother calling out, *Wolf-gangerl, Wolfgangerl, are you all right, my dear, had a good night, my dear, my darling, my star?*

And I knew, nobody had to tell me, like notes written out in black and white, that the day that had started, at least in my head, so auspiciously, would end in disappointment. I did not need to hear Papa dispatch Porta, our servant, to my protector, Baron Johann Christian Bach. My father, as was his custom, spoke out his missive as he was scribbling it. *Please ask Concert Master Bach to forgive our absence this evening at Carlisle House and at dinner later at Dean House, King's Square Court, where he and Herr Carl Friedrich Abel reside, but illness has once again prevailed. My daughter Marianne has come down with a worrisome sore throat that we dread may turn into something worse, as happened last year to our dear and invincible Wolfgang, so much so that we almost sent for a priest. And I, dear sir, am indisposed, though nothing compared to the affliction that set upon me last July after the children's performance at Mylord Thanet's mansion. We must, alas, be prudent—the boy's sickness meant the loss of all July and August, forced us to move to the purer air of Chelsea, which we could ill afford. We cannot again face, as then, the cancellation of so many appearances and such forfeiture of revenue. En fin, we cannot attend. Quick, quick, go to, make sure you do not disturb the Maestro or Herr Abel at their breakfast.*

The Allegro Molto's buoyancy had lapsed into the mournful strains of my Andante, a somber second movement that denied the playfulness of the first one. Today was not the day, tonight not the night. The ladies in their radiant dresses and feathered hats would fawn over my music but not over me, they would spin their heads this way and that, where is he, where is the little wizard, where is the sensation and prodigy of Nature who has composed this at eight, why have we been deprived of his sprightly presence? Where oh where is the marvel of the courts of Europe and of King George and Queen Charlotte, where is the little genius?

The little genius will not be there, murmured my Andante mournfully.

I burst into tears and ran to Maman in the other room and buried my head in her ample lap. She rocked herself gently, rocked me gently, took her time before lifting my face to hers and wiping the water and salt from my cheeks. "It is God's will, Wolfgang," she said. "He sent the catarrh to your sister and made your father dizzy with vertigo and made us fret about you when you were ailing last year, in February, oh February, oh cursed month. But are we to doubt His wisdom, that there is a reason why He arranges events, even those in February, according to His unknowable desires and not according to our mortal ones? Will you defy God?"

I said I would not but still, I added, why had He made me write the symphony if He was going to impede my hearing it under the insuperable baton of Maestro Bach?

"A trifle, my son. Imagine if He had decided to blind you as He did the beloved Handel, and Homer and Milton and so many in our time, then, perhaps you might ask why. Or if you were struck deaf! But this postponement of pleasure? Trust me, it will turn out for the better."

"But what if they don't like my symphony—they expected me to be there, they will have attended because they were—"

"Well then, if they are so foolish, can you guess what we'll do to them?"

I did, I did, and answered as she knew I would, accompanied by my first smile of the morning.

"We'll shit on them, Maman."

She nodded, as gratified as if I had remembered my multiplication tables. "But first, Johannes Chrysostomus Wolfgang Theophilus—"

"Amadeus!"

"But first, Amadeus, what will we do first?"

"First we'll fart at them, Maman, and then we'll shit on them."

"And then?"

"And then they can lick my ass."

"And what else?"

"Lick up all the muck on the ground."

We both laughed heartily, enjoying, more than the joke itself, the company of each other, our warmth forever.

"But maybe," Maman said, "there will be no need for such extreme measures. Maybe God will marshal some other, more satisfactory, solution for this evening."

I laughed again, wildly, raucously, grabbed a broom from the corner of the room, mounted it, and began to trot around her. Her claps and delight at my antics made me laugh again, and our joy must have been the cue for a solution to indeed make its appearance.

Presto, the answer to my troubles, my Presto, the third movement of my symphony had foretold what was going to happen if only I had been faithful enough, believed enough in my own music and Providence's hand, that there would be a happy outcome and conclusion to the grief of the Andante, nothing could keep me from the harmony I had created to make the world a more tolerable place, nothing could keep me from my audience.

Presto, the sound in the street of a presto carriage and then the presto knock at the door and the presto voice of my mentor and Maestro Johann Christian, my friend Christel—call me that, he said, but don't tell anyone, that's what they called me when I was your age, when my own father was still alive—yes, it was he, my friend was at the door.

Come to save me.

Johann Christian Bach would bear no excuses, accept no remonstrance.

He would send his carriage to fetch me as the sun went down, I would be bundled up and cared for and returned safe and sound and victorious to Thrift Street after dinner with the Earl of Thanet and his wife at Dean Street. It was to the advantage of all: young Mozart would bask in the performance of his symphony, the audience would whet its appetite with a preview of what awaited them at Nannerl and Wolfgang's benefit concert of February 21, and Carlisle House and our hostess, Mrs. Cornelys, would be enchanted that the surprise guest had shown up after all.

His voice was firm and persuasive in the midst of the bedlam rising all around us: Nannerl's sobbing because her fever was to blame for ruining this chance to consolidate our family fortune, my Papa insisting that it was an absolute *Unmöglichkeit*, impossible, impossible, the boy may catch his death of a cold and we are running out, dear friend, of black powder, Maman entreating her dear Leopold to reconsider, and of course, of course, my own shrill entreaties, not to mention Porta, who was offering coffee to our guest while the housemaid, Hannah, imperturbably made the rounds with morning scones, just out of the oven.

Papa was relenting, I could sense it.

It was the snuffbox pledged by Lord Thanet that did the trick, the promise of that gift if I pleased him enough when I played after dinner as they sipped their liqueurs. Another one, that we could place next to the silver snuffbox I had received from the Comtesse de Tessé at Versailles just last year. Lord Thanet was beckoning with it, was almost in the room with us.

"But can it not be another night?"

No, alas, Milord was leaving tomorrow for his Scottish estates and had no sure date of return.

"And it is gold, you say?"

Inlaid with gold, in and out. For the lad if he performs well, as he usually does.

"Oh he will, he will, he will perform better than he ever has. Blindfold my Wolfgang, cover the keys of the piano, ask Milady to pick any tune and watch him improvise a whole sonata on that theme—all this and more, as you well know, Herr Bach."

So it was agreed?

"You say you will bring him back at night, in the dark, when the cold is most devious, when ice lurks dangerously, no, it cannot be, we cannot risk our treasure for this one piffling chance, he is delicate and requires constant attention. You must understand, sir, today is February second. It is a heavy date in this family. Two of our boys, little Leopoldus and our own Carolus, both, both, were taken from us by God separately, on this very date, one of them, our first-born, sixteen years ago, the other, it has been exactly thirteen years since he—a portentous day, dear Kapellmeister Bach, for our sole surviving male heir to venture forth into the storm."

Perhaps the Presto was over, perhaps we were back to the Andante or something even sadder, a Requiem for my hopes, a funeral for my dreams?

Maman intervened.

"Let us discuss this no further. If your concern, Leopold, is for the heavy burden I carry, concern yourself no more, dear husband. It is Woferl and his future that we must consider. The boy shall go."

"And the cold, so late at night, upon his return, the cold, the cold?"

My mother touched my loving Papa lightly on the sleeve and turned, much to my glee, to my savior: "If it does not inconvenience you, Herr Bach, the boy could sojourn with you till tomorrow. I know your housekeeper well and she will make sure he is amply provided for. And in the morning, after breakfast, you can play the pianoforte with him, as you have intended for some time, a way for both of you to spend some pleasant hours improvising a tune or two. As long as you bring him back in time to attend Sunday Mass, dear sir."

My friend Christel winked at me and announced that, of course, Madame had shown once again her wisdom and that he had not dared to offer such hospitality for fear that it would occasion even more resistance. It was a most excellent solution—by tomorrow morning the blizzard would have waned and the ice in the streets thawed out and he would deliver me personally to my amorous and affectionate parents so young Mozart could go to Mass, a need that he, as a devout Catholic, understood all too well.

And then my sister chipped in, please, please, Papa, do not trim our Wolfgang's wings, joined by my own pleas, and that was enough—along with the golden snuffbox!—to corner Leopold Mozart.

That very afternoon he relinquished me into the tender mercies of Kapellmeister Bach with the frequent admonition to make sure I was not disturbed by marauders and scoundrels and false friends, bloodsuckers and worthless fops—the lad has a heart that is far too kind and mild—so please, dear sir, do not let him out of your sight.

How could the magnificent Johann Christian Bach keep me in his sight? Not even if he had been endowed with the thousand eyes of Argo. He was busy, he had his own patrons and admirers and pupils to placate and entice, no sooner had he completed the last compasses of the Minuetto of his latest opus than he was engulfed by a flock—or was it a swarm—of well-wishers, many of them demanding where they might purchase copies and engravings of the works they had just heard, as well as the latest six sonatas for violin and clavichord, not overly difficult on the fingers, they pleaded, so that their candid daughters would not be frustrated when they played the pieces at home.

I did not envy him the adoration.

He deserved that and much more.

His winks toward me were enough to make him the most deserving individual on the face of the earth. Winks of complicity that had commenced that morning and persisted through our carriage ride in the early evening all the way to Carlisle House in the midst of the falling softness of the snow, and had transformed themselves, during the meandering soirée, into musical winks, so subtle that not even the most discerning of the cognoscenti and habitués could have picked them up, not even his confrere and soul mate Abel, whose own suite for cello had opened the night.

Maestro Bach had organized his part of the session as a dialogue with me, almost an homage. Once the audience had gluttonously enjoyed my Symphony in E-flat Major, he had presented his own composition in the same key, as if we were associates rather than master and protégé, the Larghetto and Minuetto a reminder that I need not always end with a Presto. And then, to top the evening off, his Symphonia Concertante in C Major, inverting the order of the movements I had just entranced the public with—it had to be on purpose that my mentor opened with an Andante and then graduated to his own jolly Allegro, a tactful way of telling me that I was on the right track, boy, but there is still much you need to learn, lad, listen and follow me into fame, fame and a big fat purse.

How carefully he had left intricate clues for me, where I should press forward next, how the winds should interweave and then distance themselves from the strings and then come together again, spurring me to not let myself be held back. Oh, I was ready to learn and imitate, but that was...not enough, not enough. I hardly dared allow the thought to surface, something—could it be?—was missing in the Maestro's nocturnal offering. I did not yet know what and would not have volunteered to tell him if I had managed to articulate it to myself—something had been eliminated from his pleasant harmony, no, not eliminated, for to eliminate an emotion it must first have been expressed. The London Bach did not himself know that a certain depth was lacking, he might never know it. If there was infinite sorrow in his work it was due to what he suspected was awaiting him at the top of the mountain but could not reach and feel in all its glory, whereas I could, I could feel that infinitude, that sorrow, that gloria in excelsis. Oh, I had plumbed it in my own Andante, far less complex and elaborate than his but speaking more directly to the elusive Paradise we were both seeking.

His work was light, it was consoling, it was cheerful, it was congenial—but perhaps too much so. Too gay. The consolation had been decided before the grief had been given its time and space, the consolation was there, already guaranteed and ordained, when the piece began and was effortlessly recovered, still there, at the end. It had not changed in the interval. More disquieting yet: it had not changed me.

That was merely a child's intuition. Unarticulated then. Thirteen years later, when he and I were to meet again in Paris in more spectral circumstances, when I had seen, alas, what I had always yearned to see and yet feared, when I had seen minute by minute someone die, someone so dear, so close—when the London Bach and I met again, well, by that time I knew what was missing in his music, what my own music was already achieving, though, once more, I did not tell him this in Paris, not because I was unable to articulate it but precisely because I could, because it was enough to let my art speak for itself, my music would indicate the distance between a surface and an abyss, between a surface and the dark and luminous air stirring the stars.

There is nothing wrong with surfaces, I have skated on them often and pleasantly enough, but I was not willing to dwell there, a point there was no need to hammer home to Maestro Bach. I loved the man and he was gracious to me in return. The first truly illustrious composer to recognize me, someone whose opinions I truly valued. Not a duke whose clumsy fingers and amateurish mind slaughtered the viola da gamba while commanding entertainment. Not a prince who disbursed florins for dances that were lovely enough trifles but forgotten as soon as they had been pounded out by feet and waved into oblivion by swanlike arms. Not an Archbishop who vaunted my music because of the prestige it gave to his court.

Johann Christian Bach: someone who understood, really understood, and could teach me much that I myself ignored and also force me to realize all that he could never teach me, that, alas, I would never be able to teach him, that I could teach no one, unless... unless someone like me were to come along, is perhaps waiting for me back in Vienna when I return from Leipzig, hoping I will take him under my wing, young now, as I was then, be generous with him, as Christel was with me in London, as my Papa had always been. Will I recognize that new genius if he crosses my path? Has he even been born yet? Will he ever be born? What had Johann Sebastian thought of his own son? Did he fathom that neither this Christel nor any of his other lads would ever reach the heights and depths of his own extraordinary work? Did my own father fathom this already about me back in 1765? Did it matter to him? Did it matter to me? Only inasmuch as I have often prayed that my own dear estranged Papa never came to comprehend his own deficiency before he died, that he died in peace.

Not that all of this—in fact, hardly any of it—was in my mind that night. Only that Johann Christian had earned the right to be the center of the milling crowd, just as I merited this interlude of solitude, alone in my corner, enjoying the first unguarded evening of my existence.

And that is when the thin stranger had approached me, that is when we began to talk of secrets and rescues and...finally, once I was hooked, once I had said yes twice to his request without appraising what that nine-year-old boy was committing himself to, only then did Jack Taylor, Esquire, Physick, Eye Surgeon, of Hatton Gardens, introduce himself with another curtsy, bending his back even lower.

Which I corresponded, stating my own name.

"Jack Taylor," he insisted, "son of the Chevalier Taylor and the pious Ann King."

I nodded. "And I am the son of Leopold Mozart and Anna María Pertl, neither of whom, as you clearly have observed, is present tonight. Or you would not, I warrant, waylay me. My father might not approve."

"I have heard of your father, young sir, as you must have heard about mine."

I murmured an apology. I had no idea who this Chevalier was and wondered why it carried any weight in our proceedings. Were we to natter all night about our genealogy?

"The Chevalier Taylor," he repeated the words with intensity. "Oculist to our good King George, having attended the Kings of Poland, Denmark, Sweden, the Royal Infant Duke of Parma, the Electors of the Holy Empire, the Princes of Saxe-Gotha, Mecklenburg, Brunswick, and even your own Salzburg, known in every Court, Kingdom, Province, State, City, and Town of the least Consideration in all Europe, without exception."

He had recited this litany many times over, as a child, then as a youth, and well into his adulthood, and did so yet again, not to impress me with his pedigree but for another reason, as yet unrevealed. The lad by his side had been repeating this catalogue of titles silently to himself, lips pursed, tongue fluttering, and when his father was done added, in an English that I apprehended solely because Jack Taylor, Esquire, translated the words quietly in my ear:

"The Chevalier Taylor. Author of forty-five Works in different languages, the produce for upwards of thirty years of the Greatest Practice in the cure of distempered Eyes, of any in the Age we live."

And Jack Taylor, recurring to gnarled German, in a more forceful voice: "The Chevalier speaks many languages like a native, Italian and Swedish and Russian and, *naturellement*, French. And his German is superior to mine."

Then the boy by Jack Taylor's side muttered something else, where the only words I could extract were "books" and the number "three."

I did not wait for the translation.

If I did not interrupt this father and son duet, we would never get to the juncture where I was informed about the secret I was supposed to keep, except from the London Bach, or the mission to be undertaken. I saw the opportunity to turn the subject to Mr. Taylor himself and not his progenitor, and I politely pounced.

"Your German is outstanding, especially for an Englishman, Mr. Taylor. How long have you been studying my tongue?"

"For the past four years. Ever since our benevolent King George the Third married Charlotte of Mecklenberg-Streilitz. I have engaged in private lessons by day, crammed assiduously into the night, in the hope of someday being able to converse with Her Majesty, employing the words of her youth."

I could not contain a grimace. I had half expected him to say that I was the reason, and not the Queen, for his grinding away at my native language, that he had heard of my musical feats and set off instantly on his journey into the German tongue. Or at least since the news had been trumpeted abroad that the Mozart family had departed Salzburg in June of 1763 with London as our final destination. Jack Taylor must have read some hint of frustration furrowing my brow, because he hastened to add: "Of course, once you and your loved ones arrived on our shores last April and once I learned that Kapellmeister Bach had played for the Queen with you on his knees, the two of you improvising amazing melodies for their Royal Majesties, as was reported in the broadsides, well, I must admit that I intensified my lessons, now with the prospect of speaking to you face-to-face, an optimism that Providence has seen fit to recompense tonight. Because you are the one, you are the only one, who can save the honor of my family."

He made a flourish with his hands, like two squalid stalks in the breeze, mimicked by the boy. I had seen such extravagant fanfares in France, but none thus far in England, where gentlemen were more reserved in the expression of their feelings.

Not to be outdone, I responded with a similar display of bravado, as if the horns and drums of Lully were announcing some major event, oh, how I was enjoying myself: "If it does no dishonor to me, sir, or to my own family, I will be glad to oblige within the limits imposed by my meager age. But pray tell, Mr. Taylor, what exactly—exactly," I repeated the word, "is it you would like me to do, sir?"

For the first time, he seemed nervous. He looked around him. I followed his eyes and they lit upon the large back, like that of a bear, of Johann Christian Bach, who continued to receive the devotion of a remarkable beehive of enthusiasts.

"If we might repair to a neighboring room to partake of some refreshments, I would be more at ease to lay bare my proposal."

I hesitated. Let me confess that I hesitated. No matter how thrilled I was to be offered, on this, my inaugural night of independence, an undertaking so mysterious, I was aware that the real danger lay not in whatever Mr. Taylor might intend but in how my father might react to any mischief I was sure to get myself into, not to mention the breach of confidence regarding my friend Christel, who had solemnly sworn to keep me from any harm. It should have alarmed me that Jack Taylor, after trailing me for months, seemed so anxious to conceal his intentions from those vigilant eyes.

My curiosity prevailed.

I followed father and son to an adjacent chamber, where Taylor and I sat ourselves down on a settee of blue and yellow satin, the boy at our feet. As if I were an adult like Taylor, and his son the only child. I liked that!

Jack Taylor saw me contemplating the boy and nodded in his direction. "My son John," he said. "The third member of the Taylor men to bear the same name. John the Third, also to be an oculist. Here to assist me."

He bent down and whispered something to the lad, and I realized that young John had been clutching a satchel to his side, as if he were a messenger for some sovereign, so wary of his doubloons being stolen that he had managed to hide them from view all this while. Now he unearthed from the unobtrusive bag three unwieldy books, followed by a tidy sheaf of papers.

"This is the memoir my father published four years ago," Jack Taylor said. "It is being translated into twelve languages, one of which is German, and I would like to confer upon you a copy of the present edition, as a token of my gratitude for your willingness to assist in the task of vindicating the regard in which its author should be held."

I demurred, mumbled something about the Mozart family traveling light. Light in a manner of speaking. Papa was always worrying about how he could dispatch back to Salzburg the trunkloads of gifts Nannerl and I were accumulating, hats, medallions, swords, jewels, velvet suits, fashionable wigs, calendars made in Liege, portraits drawn in Paris, watches and watch chains and toothpick cases of all varieties, and, of course, snuffboxes, but my progenitor would have had an apoplectic fit if I had appeared tomorrow in the morning with three hefty tomes of doubtful value under my arm. Nor did I wish to brook a grilling as to their provenance. Covering one's tracks, I was discovering, might cause more problems than the existence of the original slight misdemeanor.

"Then examine these, young sir," said Jack Taylor, waving at me the documents his son had passed on to him. "Just one brief look, so I can more easily elucidate the problem prejudicially faced by my family."

I hastily perused them. Each was a testimonial to the efficacy of the Chevalier John Taylor, patent licenses from Dukes and Princes and diverse high-ranking authorities in many lands naming him their Opthalmiater, degrees conferred by the most learned Universities, pontifical decrees as to the Oculist's abilities, encomium from the cities of Florence and Bremen, membership in Royal Medical Societies.

I was impressed. They seemed authentic. Though what did I know? They could well be forgeries. But if so, Jack Taylor was taking a colossal risk, as such fraudulent claims were bound to be unmasked, thwarting his plans and leading oculist father and oculist son to be jailed for counterfeiting royal signatures. Besides, if I accepted that this was all a gigantic hoax, then my expedition was over. Better to presume that these papers professed the truth.

"And having a parent, sir, of such renown, you need my services in order to...?"

"His fame, his glory, his esteem, were unparalleled and uncontested, save for a perverse few, envious blackguards—you and your family must know all too well how envy can corrode the most exalted reputations, what conspiracies can be hatched by those with less talent, those who criticize new procedures and avenues, whether in music or in medicine—I say and repeat that my father was worthy of praise and devotion for the many ailments of the eye that he cured, the vision he restored to thousands, his unique couching method for dealing with cataracts, the forty-five books on the subject he has published. Eulogized, that is, until the year after these memoirs of the Chevalier were printed, the first dedicated to me, his only son, the second to Garrick, the eminent actor, the third to the merchants of London. Praised by all, until 1762, that is."

"Because in 1762...?"

A servant came by with tea and coffee and sweet biscuits and all three of us allowed ourselves to be pampered for a minute or so, united in the camaraderie of food and drink.

"Because in 1762...?" I repeated.

"Because in the summer of 1762, Herr Johann Christian Bach, your friend, henceforth to be celebrated as the

London Bach, stepped on English soil and began what I sadly must call an unremitting campaign against my father and his practice."

This was not what I had expected. If I had been standing, I would have backed off, as from a patient with smallpox. Being seated and boxed in by the sofa, I could only stop sipping my tea and edge away from suddenly infected Jack Taylor and son. Did they want me to side against my mentor, my host, my savior, my Christel?

Noticing my discomfort, Jack Taylor did his best to allay any fears.

"I have nothing but reverence and respect for Herr Bach. There has been a misunderstanding, that is all, and you will be the instrument, I presume, to redress that unfair situation. Because my father has been seeking an audience with Johann Christian Bach for the past two and a half years. Every request of his has been refused. Even David Garrick's good offices have been to no avail."

"It should not be so difficult," I said, still keeping my distance, setting down my cup of tea and half-bitten biscuit for emphasis. "Herr Bach is concertmaster to the Queen, and if your father, as you say, is Oculist to the King, they should chance upon each other frequently, indeed I am surprised that I did not make his acquaintance when I myself was at the court on any of my three visits."

"The Oculist to the King is only summoned to the palace when there is a medical emergency, and as our sovereign George the Third has, thank God, the eyesight of an eagle and the stamina of a stallion, there has thus been no need recently or not ever to call upon my father since his appointment twenty years ago to George the Second."

I was truly puzzled.

"He can visit Kapellmeister Bach at his home. In Dean Street. At King's Square Court. Tonight, he will be there this very night. Let him knock on the door and introduce himself and—"

"My father is abroad right now. In France. Amiens, Rheims, Rouen, in Brussels tomorrow and Amsterdam the day after. You know how grim it is to make a living in one's own land. My father has been traveling for many decades, and once it became clear to him that his offers of reconciliation were most stubbornly rebuffed by Johann Christian, he set out on yet another journey, asking me, as his most obedient son, to find a way to set up a meeting upon his return. Or if not with me, my father the Chevalier said, with you, Jack, why should he snub you?"

"And yet, sir, if you might illustrate me further as to what might have transpired between your father and my friend Baron Bach..."

Mr. Jack Taylor was becoming more agitated by the minute, keeping his voice muffled, nonetheless, wary of calling undue attention to our conversation.

"I prefer not to go into details. You are not of an age yet when you might grasp the passions that often stir in men's breasts, the bad influence that some villains exercise upon them. Suffice it to say that Maestro Bach, since his arrival in London three years ago, has poisoned the opinion of everyone he meets against the Chevalier, with manifest venom when it comes to Her Majesty, who confides in her music master, a fellow German, unreservedly. The sins of the fathers are not supposed to be visited upon their children, and yet I am also being maligned, I am being smeared without any expectation of a response."

"And you wish me to . . . ?"

"If the Maestro will not receive me in person—and I fear he is so inflexible, so hostile, that he will not relent, even if you solicit, young Master Mozart, an audience— he refuses to shake my father's hand, leaves the room if he so much as remarks the Chevalier's entrance or mere attendance—if you are unable to change his attitude, I would invite you then, and only then, mark well—to offer him the following message."

Jack Taylor waited expectantly. He clearly wished me to ask him the content of the said message.

I did so.

"Tell Maestro Bach to please inform the Queen about what really occurred between his father and my father, the truth, tell him that he need tell no one else, save the Queen, of the two operations my eminent father practiced on Johann Sebastian Bach."

"Your father operated on Herr Bach's father?"

"Twice. And the Queen needs to be informed of the truth."

"Would it not make more sense that you transmit to me the particulars of the truth you allude to, so I may apprise Maestro Johann Christian, in case he does not know it?"

"He knows it, he knows. A knowledge that, it happens, I do not possess myself, young sir, that I was never told. Only that it is not what the Kapellmeister has been whispering into the ear of Her Majesty Charlotte. The truth lies elsewhere, that I swear on all that is sacred, on the life of my mother, the pious Ann King."

"This is a strange mission," I said. "Why have you stalked me all these months to deliver a message neither you nor I understand? Why me?"

"Because this London Bach loves you well. Because an innocent child like you can assuage, as your music can, the hardest of hearts, return the Maestro to his own innocent youth when, like you, he would not have spurned someone who came with such sincerity and reticence to seek his grace."

I asked Jack Taylor if his father was a good and honest man, if he could vouch for him as I could for mine, as I could for my mentor Baron Bach.

He responded with stories that would long remain with me, he furnished several examples of his father's generosity, he mentioned his own founding of a hospital for the poor, he swore on the life of his sole male heir that there could be no doubt as to the morality and just cause of his own progenitor.

Despite the clarity of Jack Taylor's passion and the eloquence of his assurances, I needed to probe a bit more before venturing into the fire, so I could present his brief forthrightly, without qualms or uncertainty.

"And he has no defects?"

"No man is entirely blameless. But if I were to select one thing that can be criticized, the author of my days has been too liberal in his promises, he offers more out of the goodness of his heart than he or any mortal can deliver when he notices the distress of his patients. Can you not venture the same for yourself and your generous heart?"

He was playing me like a fiddle and I knew it and I did not mind. Because his assessment of me was, after all, spot-on. So I answered, yes, yes, I had been accused of a similar excess of kindness.

"You'll understand then, young sir, that what he is asking is not immoderate. Let me tell you what happened on one of my father's journeys, not far from where you were born. He was ushered into the presence of the Duke of Holstein, and he looked at the man—one of the most powerful sovereigns in Europe, right?—looked him in the face. One of the lord's chief gentlemen-in-waiting pulled at the skirts of my dear Papa's coat and warned him that he was not to take in any of his lordship's features, unless he received permission to examine his eyes for possible surgical relief. Had he forgotten his place? My father answered the acolyte vivaciously, *No, you, sir, are the one who forgets, you are forgetting that I looked last week on the King himself in the face, and shall do so with every man and any man, for we are all God's creatures.* He spoke in such a vigorous voice that the Duke heard him and praised my father as a brave fellow and said, *Look me full in the face, as you will from now on.* And that is all my father has been requesting of Johann Christian Bach—that they look each other full in the face and, therefore, full in the soul, because the eyes are the windows of the soul, the index of the mind. Is not this the sort of man who merits respect and assistance? Is it not what your own father would require of your person as you make your way into—?"

And here, he broke off.

A booming baritone emerged from the vaults of the Hall next door, above the clatter and the chatter and banter and buzz of the departing audience, the murmur of a human tide excitedly receding:

"Wolfgang! Wolfgang!"

It was Johann Christian Bach, belatedly keeping his promise to my father to keep me in his sight, suddenly aware that his young charge had vanished.

"Abel, Abel, do you know where our little scamp is hidden?"

"I thought he was with you," came Abel's slurred response, perhaps he had been drinking more than was prudent in such circumstances, though it had not hindered his cello performance one whit.

"I told you not to let him out of your sight."

"Sight, sight. The lad is to be heard and not seen. Even a blind man could find him. I'll look upstairs and you down here."

"What?" came the gruff, slightly masculine, staccato voice of Teresa Cornelys, as if she were still performing in an opera back in Italy. "Is the child lost? In my own Carlisle House? How can it be? Oh, how, how can it be?"

Jack Taylor had grown pale.

"I must hence," he said, speedily gathering the documents while his son stuffed the three volumes of his grandfather's memoirs into the satchel. "If he chances upon me here—"

"It would be an opportunity to confront him face-to-face, as the Chevalier did to the Duke of Holstein."

Jack Taylor grabbed me by the arm and his son by the other one and pulled me with them into an alcove under the stairs. I laughed with glee. Hide-and-seek, we were playing hide-and-seek. He shushed me and spoke now in a voice fainter even than before, when he had asked me if I could keep a secret:

"Meeting him now," he whispered, "would only lead to a scandal. Please rely on my judgment. It would undo all we have accomplished this evening, the three of us."

I saw the figure of Johann Christian Bach rush by, calling my name, then heard him leap up the stairs in bounds. He would soon discover I was not on the second floor.

"I must go now and you must stay. When Maestro Bach has been softened by your story and my message, a meeting can be arranged under the right circumstances."

He was already sneaking away, he and the youngest John Taylor, someday to be an oculist like father and grandfather.

"Wait! And if he does not soften up, as you suggest, what then? What do I say to him?"

Jack Taylor faltered, began debating something with himself, perhaps silently with his absent father.

Then: "Handel."

"Handel?"

"Just say that to him."

"For what purpose, pray?"

"Again, I do not know. It is what my father keeps repeating. Handel knew the truth, Handel knew the truth."

"But Handel is dead, sir, dead these six years."

"Yes, he is—or things would be different, he could bear witness that... But do not mention Handel, young sir, unless your mentor refuses your offer to set up a meeting. Only in that case. Adieu, adieu."

"When shall we see each other again, how can I—?"

"Do you think we have labored this strenuously, waited this long, to abandon you now? Before you return to your parents' residence in Thrift Street, I shall remain nearby—this I vouch—so you may deliver Baron Bach's response."

I was about to inform him that I was returning to Thrift Street tomorrow morning and not, as he doubtless presumed, this very night. I had, however, a more imperative matter on my mind.

"Wait!" Imprudently, I fastened two fingers onto his sleeve. "One more question."

He turned, sighed, unwilling to disaffect me.

"Your buttons," I said. "Where do you purchase them?"

I pointed at the gleaming buttons on his vest. They were mother-of-pearl, with a few white stones around the edge and a fine yellow stone in each center. I had seen nothing as tantalizing all night.

"My buttons? You are asking about my buttons?"

"I would have my Papa acquire some for my ensemble if you would be so good as to indicate the shop."

"You will have many buttons like this one if you deliver my message. No matter what the response. Just make sure Maestro Bach listens to you—and only mention Handel in extremis!"

And then, as swiftly as he had appeared, Jack Taylor evaporated like a magician, he and the boy.

Just in time.

Johann Christian Bach came tramping down the stairs, and, as he passed the alcove where I was concealed, I jumped out at him with a shout. Waving my elbows and braying like a donkey.

"Oh, there you are!" He hugged me. The warmth of his breast and the sweat dribbling down his cheeks were somehow comforting—this man could not possibly have been malevolent with such a fine gentleman as the Chevalier. My music wove together rivals and enemies, all of them enjoying the same pleasing sounds. How could my figure itself not bring about a similar state of concord between men who were each so eminent in their fields? I would do it! I would walk with them both, hand in hand, into the august presence of Queen Charlotte, and say, *Here they are, the best of friends. You see how easy is peace, how silly war and conflict?* And she would shower me with kisses and congratulations. *The boy is not only a genius of music, but a genius of diplomacy as well, perhaps we should name him as our ambassador in Salzburg, parley a treaty with France?*

Bach shouted up the stairs. "Here he is! Not lost at all."

"Thank heaven," came a female voice. It was Clementina Cremonini! The one and only Sabina. I had been so overcome with her performance in *Adriano in Syria* that I had heard at the King's Theatre the night before my ninth birthday that I had not dared to even say hello, so intensely did I crave that this most glorious of mezzo-sopranos would someday sing one of my songs. "Thank heaven!" she now repeated, throbbing into view. "Here was I practicing your aria, Wolfgang, *Va, del furor portate*, all week long, and how would I have felt if you did not turn up to hear me—but only after dinner, mind you. I'm starving!" She leaned into me, purred into my ear—I was grateful it was the right ear—hushing her voice in order not to offend: "Theresa is not the best hostess, she could have had something more than biscuits on hand here at Carlisle House."

I lacked the courage to meet her eyes. That throat of hers! And from inside it my own song would soon ascend.

"Madame, you do me honor," I said, kissing her outstretched hand. But in my intellect I was letting slip the words she would soon sing and that I had stolen from the pasticcio *Ezio*, the very same words by Pietro Metastasio that Maestro Bach had flattered with his melodic strains, I let them slip through my mind but not my lips: *Go forth, transported by fury, remember, ingrate, who the traitor is, disclose the deception*...Was there a portent in those words I had put my own music to, a warning I should heed? Was I right to have agreed to deceptively conspire against my friend?

"You must be as famished as I am, child," she said. "Food first, then music. His music, your music. Come, Christel, let's go."

"Indeed." He took me by the hand and we headed for the cloakroom as he called out stentorously: "Abel! The boy is found. He is found, I say. And we are leaving, my friend."

A roar of approval greeted this news. Carl Friedrich Abel lumbered up to us, handsome as ever, clutching two women, one in each of his long arms. "Ah, you little scoundrel. In what closet were you hiding? And with whom, huh?"

"By myself, sir," I responded.

"Well, that leaves more for me, doesn't it?" He laughed and imparted something, which I did not catch, to his companions.

The one to his left, with more feathers adorning her than if she had been a peacock, addressed me in English. Abel shook his head and breathed a few words into her delicate ear, and she promptly lapsed into French:

"You dear boy, you dear, dear, dear little imp," she said, liberating herself from Herr Abel's embrace and planting two wet kisses on both my cheeks. "Those exquisite blue eyes!"

I think she meant it. Back then, my skin had not been disfigured yet by smallpox and my small stature was natural in someone so young—though I was already conscious of my slightly askew, malformed left ear and my prominent nose, too large for my squinty face, but I believed that she did indeed find me beautiful, that everybody did.

She made sure I did not waver in my belief.

"Ah, if you were but a bit older, dear, dear boy."

"Then he wouldn't have time to copy out my Symphony in E-flat, eh? How's that going? Learning something, boy?"

"I'm enjoying it, Herr Abel."

"As long as you don't weaken and ruin your eyesight, boy, like Christel's father. He spent the nights of his youth studying by candlelight, duplicating his elder brother's trove of musical scores with only the light of the moon through a narrow window, ha! Whereas I spent my fledgling nights in more pleasurable pursuits, eh, Johann Christian, wasted my eyesight on other nocturnal splendors. So, no copying at night if you know what's good for you, young Mozart."

"Yes, sir. I had hoped to have the copy ready for you today, except that my sister was indisposed and I have been taking care of her."

"Your father"—Abel turned again to Johann Christian—"would never have accepted that as an excuse, would he? Even if I had had a sister nearby. Not that any of my sisters would have entertained me as much as other ladies did back then. Though I was a bit older than this tiny, marvelous Wolfie creature when I was apprenticed in Leipzig, eh? Left a few years after you were born, Christel, but the wenches there, right, they cannot have changed that much, eh? Sweeter than a cello, wouldn't you say?"

"Enough of this nonsense," said Johann Christian, nervously patting a disobedient strand of hair under his wig.

"Nonsense? Nonsense?" came the good-humored response. "You dare to treat me thus, when I held you on my knee when you were tinier than this lad here and fed you half of my sweets? And you exist, after all, because my father brought your parents together. My partner, Clementina"— and he turned to her—"doesn't like to be reminded that it was my father that whispered to his, *She's the one, Anna Maria Magdalena is the one*, helped him choose her as future wife and mother to Christel. And how does he repay that my family allowed him to exist? By daring to accuse me, me, of nonsense."

"Very well, then, it is not nonsense," responded my mentor, affectionately. "But this much is certain: dinner is getting cold, and you know how I hate it when the pudding is not warm."

"It's warm enough here," Abel commented. "Only one fire at home in the dining room hearth at Dean Street while here, as you can see for yourself…"

"Stay, then—and reassure Theresa Cornelys that the boy is found and Clementina and I have absconded, that I thank her for such magnificent hospitality and shall come by tomorrow to review the receipts and settle any outstanding accounts."

Abel promised to follow as soon as humanly possible. "I will bring Polly, dear friend, Polly is always good fun."

"Just don't bring her uncle or François Hyppolite," came the reply. "They would spoil the evening."

A tall, lugubrious dandy stopped at that instant to flatter the Maestro on his playing.

"We were just speaking of my father," Johann Christian said. "He was of the opinion there was nothing remarkable in his playing, which I can assure you was supremely better than mine. It is a matter, he said, of hitting the right notes at the right time, and the instrument does the rest."

The man reddened, his face like a herring, and muttered something about the modesty of geniuses and was gone. My mentor turned to the rose-cheeked lass who had been holding our coats and furs and headgear for a while now. He murmured a compliment to her, inaudible, though clear in intention. She blushed and curtsied.

As we bundled up, Johann Christian Bach said to me: "So, lad, I could see you were keeping something from our friend Abel, but not from me, I trust. What mischief have you really been up to, all this time?"

"Oh, nothing much."

"What? No adventures? No damsels in distress? No ogres that require a good trouncing?"

"Merely a passing conversation that might interest you, sir, that I will detail when time and solitude discreetly allow."

"A wise decision, isn't that right, Clementina? Secrets can wait. Good company cannot, nor can a lavish supper. And Lord Thanet has been at Dean Street cooling his heels—on a night like this—for an hour! And he has brought the snuffbox!"

We made our way out, the three of us, through a tumult of ladies and gentlemen. As we swept down the steps of Carlisle House, I caught a glimpse of Jack Taylor and son lurking in a shadow across Soho Square. Just enough light from the flurry of snow shimmering off a hundred candles and a dozen torches to illuminate the glint of their eyes, despondent because of the cold they were braving, hopeful because they believed I would bring their family nightmare to an end.

I wondered, as I clambered into the carriage, if I was old enough and had enough courage to do so; I wondered if I would find a way to speak to Baron Bach about a subject he might find distasteful and not end up banished from his presence, as he had banished the Chevalier for a sin that had yet to be revealed.

That's what I wondered as we started out into the storm, crossing the streets that only a few years earlier the great George Frideric Handel had walked, the streets he could no longer visit, Handel, who was now part of my new secret universe, part of a mystery that I did not know then it would take me many years to unravel, that even now, as I stand in front of Johann Sebastian's tomb in Leipzig, even now I am not sure I have yet fully understood.

SECOND CHAPTER

London, February 2–3, 1765

Adagio

I was unable to reconcile sleep that night at Johann Christian's home on Dean Street. Not merely the day's excitement. Something of greater morbidity dogged me: the image of my two little brothers kept creeping into my thoughts, scratching like a soreness in the throat. Just my imagination, that scrabbling in my vocal cords. Still, I was assailed by the wild idea that God might come for me, as He had come for them. Why was I breathing, sniffing, eating, shitting, composing, playing the harpsichord, playing the violin, basking in plaudits, why was I discerning the shape of the snow as it fell reflected on the ceiling, improvising the next sonata, touching the smooth field of the sheets, feeling the pillow fluff under my head, why, why,

why was I the one wide-awake in this bed in London and they were dust in Salzburg? We had occupied the same space inside our mother, I had grown in the darkness they had known before me, I had escaped that sweet darkness and followed them out into the world. Except that I had remained here and they had left it.

Maybe it was now my turn to die, punishment for flaunting my father's admonishments, for hiding my designs from my mentor Johann Christian, for responding to my mother's kindness with disobedience.

I calmed myself, recalling how splendidly the evening had gone, how the Almighty had bombarded me with bounty, not forgetting to add the snuffbox as a prize at the end.

A reward richly deserved—and earned! Not only by playing the piano after dinner, every trick my Papa had promised I would display, play and display, the reason I was there at Dean Street. Not just my musical performances. Other performances, games to be played as adroitly as a viola, all executed cheerfully and yet with a sense of foreboding, the knowledge that at some point the assembly of personages sitting around the table first and then in the drawing room would dissolve, as all audiences dissolve eventually, and leave us alone, myself and Maestro Bach. Then I would have to cease games and music and become the messenger, perhaps endure his wrath at my mission, perhaps he would consider it treachery to have merely entertained an overture from his enemy.

Fabulous and grand, everything should have been that night, albeit colored by Jack Taylor's pleading eyes and reed-like voice, everything unnerved by the faraway Chevalier—monster or saint?—I was never to meet.

Is that true? Am I remembering it all well?

Did I recall the Chevalier when they served the roast capon, the liver dumplings, the trout smothered with almonds, the truffles, the chocolates? Was Jack Taylor troubling me when we all sat down at the table, Abel and his latest conquest, the ravishing Polly Young, and Christel and the divine singer Clementina, whose hand I had kissed a few minutes ago in Carlisle House, oh what a company it was, better still when we were joined by Giovanni Manzuoli, the famed castrato who had been giving me sublime singing lessons for the last few months—what a distinguished group, convened by Lord Thanet, owner of the snuffbox and owner of our time and owner of the large purse that would pay for the dinner, though it was his wife, Lady Thanet, who opened the festivities by flamboyantly proposing a diversion.

"*Moments Musicaux*," she said in French.

It was the language they had all agreed on, the first game of the evening: What Shall We Speak So No One Is Left Out? German was verboten, as only three of us (myself, Abel, and Bach) spoke that devilishly difficult (according to Milord Thanet) tongue. English was out of the question, as neither I nor Manzuoli was fluent enough in it. Manzuoli recommended Italian, of course, the language of opera and the Scarlattis, essential to anyone musically inclined, but

Milady would have none of it, murmuring in an aside that she had never wanted to learn it, that barbarous degeneration of Latin. Clementina, always ready to amuse herself by stirring up trouble, quickly translated the insult to Manzuoli, who stood up violently, exclaiming: *"Ma non è possibile, questa donna c'è una calamitá."* He departed in a huff—and sorry though I was to see my song master leave, I had to admit that, given his hot temper and perpetual desire to harvest all attention, it may have been a blessing, perhaps Milady Thanet had provoked him on purpose so I should be the main attraction, because later in the evening I heard her exchange jokes with Clementina...in Italian!

At any rate, as soon as the door slammed behind the erratic castrato, the rest of the troupe settled on the language of Molière and Rameau as best suited for our merriment, though not one among us had been born in France.

Which was why Her Ladyship had pronounced the words *Moments Musicaux*, which even Maman, who spoke not a word of French, would have understood.

"I can count in our circle," she said, with a sweeping gesture of her lovely pale arm, "five esteemed practitioners of music. Each of you must tell us how and when and wherefore you first heard the sweet sounds that have become your profession. The earlier the memory, the more moving, will determine the winner."

"And who shall judge if it is to be moving?" asked Polly Young, extricating her hand from the amiable clasp of the London Bach.

And at that moment, greeted by a roar of laughter, who should stroll in, straight from their large, adjacent mansion on Kings Square Court, who could it be but Mr. Domenico Angelo and his pretty young wife, Elizabeth, almost dancing in, as if ready to give each and every one of us a fencing lesson—oh, he had offered to teach me swordsmanship for free, because you wield the saber of your music so adroitly already, young Wolfgang—and the one who smiled most at this appearance was Lady Thanet, who exclaimed, "Eh, voilà, here are our judges! They will decide the victor, the person who will receive this watch chain"—she dangled it from a bottle of wine—"and a kiss from me if a gentleman; if a lady, a kiss from my husband. If a child, a kiss from us both. What say you?"

"Must the stories be true?" I asked, and everybody laughed.

"My wife," announced the Earl of Thanet, "follows Aristotle in this. Better that the stories seem true than that they be true."

"Though if seeming and truth coincide, fiction and history, so much the better," added Angelo. And he winked at me, which gave me hope that this man, so often in demand to preside over competitions and invariably praised for his fairness, would rule in my favor. Oh yes, I would soon add that gleaming watch chain to my collection! And his wife Elizabeth loved music, having, it was rumored, an attractive, gentle voice, in which she had told me when I had visited them at their house on King's Court Square that I had to compose an aria for her, only for her. How auspicious, then, that this admirer of mine was the one who now opened the tourney.

"Ladies first. Clementina, *mia cara*..."

"Very simple. As a child—perhaps I was two, perhaps three years old—in Venice, my nurse would take me on strolls, past the Ospedale della Pietà. And I would hear the chorus of children, the foundlings, singing behind its walls—so it must have been Vivaldi whose works I first heard, who started me on my career, though I never met that most superb of composers and never will, never will."

"Vivaldo?" asked Milady Thanet, frowning. "The man has fallen out of favor, I believe, since he died—when was it, fifteen years ago, more?"

"In Vienna," responded Clementina, "poor and forgotten, buried in a pauper's grave, the Red Priest he was called because of the fiery color of his hair. He should never have left Venice, never have tried his fortunes in Vienna, a city that does not appreciate the truly great."

"Not appreciate the truly great?" protested Milady Thanet. "Not so, not so. This Vivaldo—or whatever his name may be—was just a fleeting fashion. Not like Telemann, whose music will live on through the ages. What I find alarming, Clementina, is that such an extraordinary singer as yourself should owe her artistry to someone with such scant talent, this Vivaldo justifiably left behind by our modern times." Before Clementina could object that the future would have a different judgment regarding the Red Priest's greatness, Her Ladyship had moved loftily on: "How about you, Polly, our sole competitor born on this island kingdom?"

"Handel." Polly breathed that one word fervently. "I was five years old and already had a voice that enchanted the birds. *You must come with me to Covent Garden,* my father said. *To see a pageant? Nay, an oratorio.* Samson. *It is most tragic and magnificent, but appropriate for a child, as the wicked are punished and the virtuous prevail.* Handel was conducting. I saw him, I heard him, I fell in love, with him, with his music, with all music."

"Ah, yes, that must have been in 1743, when *Samson* played for the first time," Abel said, and was about to add something else when Polly flapped an impatient hand to signal that her narration was not over.

"After the concert, I ran toward Handel, my father could not stop me. *Papa Handel,* I cried out, *Papa Handel, I loved that,* and he turned and lifted me up into the air. *And you, my girl with the flaming hair? What will you be when you grow up?* And I answered, *A singer, Papa Handel, I will sing your songs when I grow up. Like Kitty Clive. She also has red hair like me, and I will sing like she does. But I will be good, not like Delilah!* He was not, I recall, a jolly man, and had no children of his own, but my enthusiasm brought on the semblance of a smile. *Good!* he exclaimed. *It is time we had more English singers and fewer from Italy, though I am still somewhat partial to Signora Avolio. I intend henceforth, except for castrati, to hire for my oratorios only subjects of our good King George. We must prove to Milan and Venice that London, my fire-haired child, is the new center of the world."*

This patriotic ending was politely applauded by everyone. Save Clementina Cremonini, who wrinkled her exquisite nose in evident irritation at this new slight to her homeland, the third of the evening.

"Handel said something similar to me," Abel interposed as the clapping faded away. "A bit before he died. I had arrived in London on March twenty-first—the year was 1759—black and blue and bruised and dizzy from the long journey from Paris, but still I betook myself to Covent Garden to—look for Polly! No, no, a joke! To listen to that self-same oratorio you first saw as a child, Polly. I hoped, of course, that he would be there, Handel, and he was, blind, seated at the harpsichord, not missing a cue, improvising from beat to beat, listening to the music he had written for poor biblical Samson, betrayed by his lover, enslaved by his enemies, redeemed only in death. He identified, perhaps, with Samson, blind and eyeless in Gaza. And when the tenor who sang his desolate aria reached the words *Total eclipse—no sun, no moon / All dark amid the blaze of noon,* I started to—I started to—"

And here, a tear dropped from Abel's left eye. Polly reached across the table and took his hand in two of hers. I could feel a similar glistening in my own orbs.

"Tears ran down every cheek in the hall." Abel recomposed himself. "Every cheek but his. He sat there, impassive, tapping his feet to the music, triumphant, like Samson, over his enemies, even over infirmities and death. I approached him afterward, as you had so many years earlier, Polly, and dared to invite him to my own concert to be held six days later, on March twenty-seventh. And he came."

"How did you manage that?" asked Elizabeth, the young mistress Angelo. "He was dying. Those were his last weeks on this earth."

"I mentioned that my mentor and teacher, the elder Bach, had asked me to convey his regards and respect if ever I had the good fortune of meeting the estimable Handel. It was a lie, of course. Your father never said anything of the kind."

"He might have," interposed Johann Christian, pensively.

"To you, perhaps, but not to me. But how was Handel ever to know the truth? How do we ever know what really happened in the past that we have not personally witnessed? And even in that case, so much is blurred by time and uncertainty. But, to the point: what mattered is that my ruse did the trick. *I shall come*, Handel said. And he did. And afterward praised my playing and even the slight *petit rien* I had composed for my first London presentation. And then invited me to hear the *Messiah* on April sixth—the last time he ever heard it, ever participated on the organ. And that very night of his last *Messiah*, he asked me to visit him at Brook Street. *Come by Thursday the twelfth*, he quipped, as he insisted that by Friday he would be dead. *It is my intention to meet my good God, my sweet Lord and Savior, on the day of his resurrection.* He was only off by one day. He expired on Saturday the fourteenth, 1759."

"And was he reconciled to his death then?" Polly asked.

"*It must be so*. One of the last things he said to me at that strange encounter—he was fading fast and would never again rise from his bed. *It must be so*. He had a young lady sing the words to him. I think he was at peace."

"Let us pray so!" intervened Johann Christian. "Generous Handel! You owe your vocation to him, Polly, and you, Abel, his praise, but I owe him my current position at the court, which used to be his. Our German Queen Charlotte has told me of how well Handel spoke of me—and his opinions must have kept tingling in her ears after his death, they were decisive, I am sure, in my assignment as her *Maître de Musique*."

Handel! Three mentions of Handel in a row! Reminding me of the mission Jack Taylor had charged me with, that I should mention his name to Christel if all else failed. Maybe I could innocently coax some more information from this opportunity, gauge if there was any danger in eventually bringing up Handel's name, but I did not manage even a word, as Maestro Bach had not finished his reminiscence: "I am honored," he said, "to be Handel's heir, so to speak. Though more honored, perhaps, to be the son of my father, Sebastian."

"Sebastian, you say?" inquired Lord Thanet. "I do not know his music, and I flatter myself on having some musical taste, wouldn't you all agree? But I am open to unknown composers, I am tolerably indulgent. Someday, Herr Bach, you must play one of your father's ditties and capriccios for me. As he sired you, he cannot entirely lack talent. Perhaps when we return from Scotland?"

"Why wait so long, Milord? Young Mozart can play you something from my father's *Art of the Fugue* this very night, after dinner. What say you, Wolfgang?"

"I'm honored to play anything by your father, sir," I answered, "or any other member of your family, as many as you command."

"There are one hundred and sixty-some Bachs who have written music, going back five generations," responded my mentor, "and thus we must be respectful of our distinguished audience and stick to one or two samples."

"Oh, it will be a delight," said Domenico Angelo, "it must be. As he was a friend of Handel's, was he not, Christian, a close and dear friend, though Lord Thanet does not know him?"

A pained, arrested expression crossed over Bach's face.

"No, they never met, Handel and my father."

"So you keep claiming," Abel exploded. He had been unusually quiet since recounting Handel's last words. He now emptied the large goblet of wine he had been nursing. "I, for one, do not believe it."

"I can assure you, my dear Abel, that it was not for want of interest on my father's part, of that I am certain."

"What? Were they not born one month apart, and in neighboring cities, not forty miles from each other, Handel in Halle and your father in Eisenach, if I am not mistaken? Why, they almost shared the same wet nurse, they must have crossed paths as children, as lads, as men—I can assure you they were on the most intimate terms. Your father, my teacher, lived, what, sixty-nine years?"

"Sixty-five," said Christel. Fleetingly, I saw something spread in him that I had not remarked before. He was a jovial man, though not exempt from solemnity, a certain Teutonic gravity when the occasion warranted it, but sadness, no, I had never seen sadness welling inside him—nor the more surprising rage that for an instant now invaded his features and just as promptly disappeared. "If he had died at sixty-nine my life would have been different indeed."

"Sixty-five years, right, and you say he and Handel never so much as glanced at each other for one second over a span of sixty-five years?"

"Destinies can be entwined, get entangled and twisted together without one man ever touching, ever seeing, ever being in the presence of another," Christian concluded, broodingly. "Murder and love and calamities and weddings make mates of perfect strangers. But this is not a subject I care to dwell on, particularly on such a festive night."

"A festive night indeed," cried out Abel, keen to shift his younger comrade and partner out of his somber mood. He showed one of the servants his empty goblet, indicating the need for more wine. "What better words to introduce my story, my own *moment musicale*—and it stars your father as well as my own father, Ferdinand, very alive and hearty, both of them dear friends at the time, so much so that Sebastian became godfather to my sister Charlotta.

Charlotta! Oh, I must go and visit her soon, I really must, oh dear."

His evident distress made me think of my own sister, ailing at that very moment, perhaps praying for things to go well for me and the family fortunes this evening. I wondered if Abel's sister might also be ill like Nannerl, and that was the reason why he had to rush back and see her. See her where? I didn't get to ask. His concern was already dissipating, so eager was he to proceed with his riotous tale.

"You asked for evidence of truth, Mr. Angelo, Mrs. Angelo. Thus far our fair contestants have been vague. But I can tell you the exact date of my essential musical encounter: January fifth, 1728, when I had barely turned four years of age. Father Bach had left Coethen before I was born, in order to become Kapellmeister in Leipzig. He still retained, however, the title of Court Composer to Prince Leopold of Anholt, and thus now and then visited with Anna Magdalena, Christian's future mother, in order to perform concerts. But I had not heard him or met him—or at least do not recall the event—until that January eve. Sebastian arrived without his wife that morning, and that may explain why, by the time his concert was scheduled to start, he had imbibed a massive amount of wine, as had my father, Ferdinand, and his brother, a landscape gardener by the name of Johann Christoph who has, alas, been long gone these many years."

"Another of your tavern tales," said Polly, pinching Abel lightly on the arm. "Cheater! You must have made this one up."

"Not at all. I tell you Father Bach had brought two cases of Rhine wine with him—and three bottles of brandy, of which he was also fond, am I right, Christian?"

"He drank modestly," replied the London Bach. "But I have seen him down several bottles and never be the worse for it."

"That's the point, that is precisely my point! They had dispatched almost all the bottles and were making merry, and then the hour came to perform. My mother was not well that day and could not accompany them, so she said to me, *Go, Carl, my love, go with your father and his friend Sebastian, and make sure they arrive safely at the Hall and come back sound as well.* I had heard, I must have listened to much music in that household since my birth, of that I am certain, but that was the first time I remember ever having attended a full, formal concert, Bach on the harpsichord and my father on the cello. Off we went into the night—it was snowing, as it is now in our London, and…and I learned a lesson about music then that I have never forgotten."

"What lesson?" I asked, breathlessly. Indeed, I was so exhilarated that my hand, which had already thus far folded the corner of the napkin into tiny pleats, now began the same process with the tablecloth itself, torturing and crumpling its edge.

"They performed better with the drink in them than if they had been sober, that is the lesson I learned. That we have but one life and we would do well to drink and eat and love our way through it as we sing for our supper, that we should never postpone the pleasure of the mouth or the flesh because we are paid to perform for the rich and powerful. If you, Milord Thanet, can drink your fill before my concert, then so can I, so can I!"

"Let's drink to that," agreed Thanet with a chuckle, lifting his cup and gesturing to a servant to fill all the glasses, save mine, to the brink.

"Yes, the worms are coming," thundered Abel, "the worms are coming for us all, but not until we have given them something to feast on, eh? Eh, boy? Never let despair seize you by the throat. Before the last trumpet will call us from our various pleasures, we will have tooted our horn, what say you?"

"I don't like trumpets," I answered. "They scare me. Even if Andreas Schachtner, trumpeter to our Prince Archbishop, is my best friend and the finest fellow that ever lived."

Again, my response was cause for hilarity, with the exception of Johann Christian Bach, who looked at me with a tender gaze.

"I also," he said, "lived in fear of loud instruments, especially the organ that my father would play with such verve and skill. Though that is not the core of my story. As with Abel, music had always been there, surrounding me, my father's hymns and stirring cantatas and entrancing strings, but none of this counts as a first moment, an event that held for me a lesson, though one different from the sort my friend Abel has so ably depicted in the hope of bribing his way to Milady's watch chain that his eyes and fingers covet, so he may pawn it and buy yet more pleasures."

"Bribing? Bribing, did you say? Are you accusing Domenico Angelo of being anything but the paradigm of virtue and justice, our arbiter, umpire, judge, fencing master, lord of good taste, party host supreme?"

"There you go again, but flattery this time will not get you the award, because my story is more moving, I wager, dear Carl, than yours. I was saying when I was so uncouthly interrupted that the moment I recall exists in real time. This was in 1740 and, like Abel, I was not yet five. My sister Johanna Carolina was two years old, and she was crying. It was such a grief-stricken keening that it could waken the dead out of pity, as if she knew at that young age what was in store for her. I had been passing the closed door of the chamber where she lay whimpering, and I opened it slightly to see if I might be of some assistance. And then I heard two other sounds. One was the trill of a linnet that my mother kept in a cage, that my father had acquired as a gift because she loved birds beyond anything in the world, save my father himself, save perhaps yellow carnations—the linnet, I say, was singing and keeping time, it seemed, with her long brown tail. I stepped into that chamber and saw my mother approach the cage and join the finch with her own melody, and as the two of them, my mother and the linnet, ascended their song like wings into heaven, the girl began to quiet down, ceased to mourn what she did not yet know awaited her, became reconciled to life and heartache, began to gurgle in delight."

"And you?" asked Clementina. "What did you do? Did you sing as well, did you turn the trio into a quartet, dear Herr Bach?"

"I left the room, closed the door, went away, plugged up my ears. I knew I had never received such a song from her. Or I would have remembered it. I had not received one like that, I say, nor ever would. I understood that if I desired that kind of harmony I would have to produce it myself, I would have to fill the world with wonder. That is the lesson I learned. My home was elsewhere. My father was too busy with his own endless tribute to a stern Lutheran god, and my mother was too entranced by her bird and her daughters. I grew up at that moment, music turned me into an adult though I was not yet five. I envisaged the man I was to be, he who performed at Carlisle House this evening, he who will perform with our young Mozart later tonight, he who speaks these words right now, he who works in order to live and not lives in order to work, he who will never, not ever, go back to his place of birth."

Total silence from all the adults greeted Master Bach's revelation. My gasp was, therefore, even more audible. What he had related was so far from any experience I had gone through or even envisaged that, yes, I gasped. Meaning the breath left me in a rush, I emptied myself of anything but bafflement and awe, so inconceivable was it that one could be that distant from one's parents or one's sister, that one could forever accept self-exile from our place of birth.

They all could not fail to notice my reaction.

And turned to me.

Perhaps they also were so affected by my mentor's story that they wished to escape it, wished me to help them escape its implications, expected their little prodigy of Nature to save them from the frailties of human Nature.

This was not how I had planned my own tale. I was intent on gaining the watch chain, on charming them all into awarding me first prize, but I realized now that my original idea was not as excellent as I had visualized. The truth is that my first encounter with music—or so I liked to tell myself, so I keep telling myself this story all these decades later as I look back and re-create my past—had been from inside my mother, an earlier memory by far than any of the four contestants who had preceded me, I had learned about the concord of the universe from her heartbeats that I still carried with me. But on several occasions that evening the company had been entertaining themselves at my expense—not maliciously, but merely because . . . well, for what other purpose was a child there among all those men and women but to amuse them? And if I were to reveal to these adults this secret of my existence, the origin of music in the very womb we all come from, the music that most mortals forget but that I was privileged to recall—if I were to blurt this out, I might receive the watch chain but I would also receive questions of all kinds, meant to be witty but in rather poor taste, I was sure. And how did you get into that womb, pray? And how did you get out? And who placed you there? Surely you have memories from before you arrived inside your mother, what canals did you navigate, through which tubes did you journey to disembark there?

No, I would not soil my recollection of that tranquility with their jests.

Instead, I stood up and walked to the clavichord that had been placidly hearkening to me since my arrival at Dean Street. The keyboard knew what I was going to do, it welcomed me in black and white, the black notes on white paper where I had, one day before I was five, made magic for the first time. My father had not believed it when my sister told him who had composed that tune, not even when I improvised a variation. *Whose melody?* he asked. *How can it be?* he asked. *Play it again*, he said. And then he was weeping, my Papa was weeping, he called my mother in and she too began weeping.

And now, they, the ladies and gentlemen who had found me so funny and droll, they were all weeping, the whole gathering.

I stood up from the instrument, took a little bow as if I did not wish for any applause, went back to the table.

"My first sonata," I said. "Written when I was still four years old. My first encounter with music."

They allowed themselves then some animation, the ladies petted me, the gentlemen tapped me on the back, there was a general buzz of delight.

Only Bach was quiet.

When the excitement had subsided, he asked: "And that melody you just played—from where did you bring it? Did you have it with you, waiting, crouching inside, since birth? Since before your birth?"

It was as if my mentor could read my mind, knew that the real memory, the real question, went far deeper into the origins of everything than what my first sonata had evoked, was forcing me to acknowledge that I had used this bravura performance in order not to risk bringing my secret of the womb out into the open air.

I answered the truth, though not all of it.

"I don't know," I said.

He wasn't going to let the matter go that easily.

"Because that is as close to God as you will ever get, child. And you remember it, bless you, with the same purity with which you lived it. I am telling you that you saw the face of God that day, without knowing it. Ah, if you were ever again to repeat that experience as a mature man, as an adult, if ever..." He lapsed into silence.

I did not know what to say.

Abel did, he had explained what lesson he derived from music and intended not to forget it.

"Enough talk of angels and clouds," he cried out. "We are here to celebrate, not to take Holy Communion. I mean, dear Bach, do you know any man who has come even close to what you are suggesting, any man at all?"

My friend Christel sighed. "One man perhaps. One man and perhaps two," he said. "But you are right. That is not where this game should lead us. The question before our judges is, who gets the watch chain?"

And, of course, I won.

Me. Woferl. Wolfgangerl. Wolfgang Chrysostomus Amadeus Mozart. The lover of God.

Later, in bed, I asked myself if the outcome had not been organized by a human hand. Not a reward preordained by my performance or the excellence of my memory, but arranged by the cunning of my friend and savior Johann Christian Bach. When Mrs. Angelo had announced the winner and Milady Thanet had given me the watch chain along with a resounding kiss—two, in fact, one on either cheek—I caught a glance of complicity between the Maestro and the Earl, an indulgent smile. And thus, perhaps, they had known all along that I would win, had convinced everyone to play the game to the hilt so that my victory would not look inevitable, so I would not feel humiliated.

Could a man that kind have conceived a malevolent disliking of the Chevalier?

I decided that I should abandon this enterprise, forgo Jack Taylor and his injured father and his insignificant son. Why should I complicate my life precisely on this night of independence, when everything had rolled along without incident or accidents of any sort? Did I not deserve, tonight and always, smooth sailing? Why risk disaffecting my mentor?

But as soon as these thoughts assaulted me, I felt again the frisson of what it meant to strike out into uncharted territory, even the guilty thrill of possibly betraying Bach's trust and my father's version of the perfect boy I was supposed to be. Was I really willing to promise that I would never engage in any mischief, never unravel the mystery posed by Jack Taylor? Never find out why the London Bach was so determined to destroy the good name of a good man?

Because the Chevalier was a good man, of that I was also confident.

There in bed, my attention returned to the reports his
son had recounted and that I had trusted but a few hours
ago. How, on the road to visit a great court, he had treated
a poor shopkeeper's daughter and corrected defects in her
vision and, seeing her indigence, did not charge her one
pfennig, and then, upon arriving at the court, was made to
wait two days until he was received by the ruling sovereigns
and, to his consternation, found himself in the presence of
the princess who was the very impoverished maiden whose
eyesight he had restored with such success and such meager remuneration. How he had given eternal happiness to a
noblewoman who was fair on one side of her face and fright-
ful on the other, and in an operation never practiced since
before Adam and Eve, he had made her equally handsome
on both sides. How a nobleman, infirm and of advanced
years, had offered the Chevalier compensation for curing
his blindness and the Great Oculist had requested that the
old man donate to a church a statue of Our Lady of Lo-
reto, all in silver, as a way of thanking God, from whom the
Chevalier derived all his dexterity. How, in Prague, discovering that an ancient and rich gentleman on his deathbed
was squandering his fortune on an unworthy and libertine
son and disinheriting a more humble but quiet male descen-
dant, repaired the old man's sight for a few hours in an intervention that had never been attempted before or since,
and that this miracle allowed the dying gentleman to see
the truth of that iniquity and leave his legacy to the good
child. And finally Jack Taylor had underscored his father's

encouragement in the founding of a hospital for the indigent blind and, when there were not enough charitable subscriptions to allow for this free service, had helped him set up such assistance for the needy to visit Hatton Gardens, where young Mozart and his family could come any day they so wished to remark for themselves the bountiful heart of the father and the diligence of the son.

What had changed between that moment, earlier in the evening, when I had been persuaded to act on behalf of this venerable surgeon and now, when I seemed consumed by fear that abetting him would be to my detriment? Did I believe less in his integrity? Did I think a man who restored so many to behold the glories of the sun, delivered them from perpetual night, did not deserve my assistance? Was I a coward, a weather vane to be buffeted hither and yon by each arbitrary, emotional gust of wind?

And was not this what I needed to learn tonight, a lesson as important as the ones Bach and Abel had each absorbed at an early age, God wanted me to trust my own judiciousness and discernment in orienting any future acts, prepare for the day when my father would be gone and my mother taken by Our Savior's grace and my sister married to some distant stranger, prepare myself for the loneliness and confusion I was now experiencing?

My discomposure was aggravated by Papa's absence. It unhinged me, to be deprived of the bedtime song he would croon in my ear every night—full of nonsense verses to a tune composed by myself, it lulled me toward sleep. And I missed his kissing me on my large nose after the last note had melted away. No, no, I would never be without him, I would keep him in a glass cage and preserve him forever, and my mother too, and honor them in their old age and shower them with riches, and if we were to die, we should do so all of us together, so neither I nor Nannerl would be left to fend for ourselves. But God would not be so benevolent to me if I failed to do what was right, if, out of weakness of character, I did not keep my promise to Jack Taylor. Yes, I would fulfill my mission. Or what sort of adventure was this, to end with the hero too scared to get out of bed?

How soon, how soon, would my mentor be back to bid me a good night so we could talk?

Now that I had reached a decision, I could not wait— and even less was I able to sleep.

I could hear the sounds from the party at the Angelo house next door, there on King's Court, wafting raucously through the winter air, across the snow-filled courtyard and the frozen garden. I imagined my friends congregated there, full of joy, in the company of so many others, Garrick and Gainsborough and Sir Joshua Reynolds, Sheridan and Cipriani and Samuel Johnson, all those illustrious guests of Domenico and his pretty young wife, Elizabeth. Then a woman's voice came to me above the din and merriment, lamenting something in Italian, "*Non so d' onde viene*," she did not know where that tender sentiment was coming from, did not like the cold iciness running through her heart, she was addressing her lover in the aria, and then the steady, unmistakable hum of Johann Christian's viola da gamba answered that sorrow, playing with it, consoling it, telling the sad woman—it was Clementina! it had to be her!—that she was not alone, telling me that I was the one who was alone, telling me that I was not old enough to be there, be one of them.

They had all gone there, the whole band, leaving me behind, all of them agreeing that I had had enough stimulation for one night. I had remonstrated and pleaded to no avail. Mrs. Angelo, despite having sworn she was my ally and that I should compose something for her, only for her—she stated that their own son, Henry, a year older than I, had been asleep four hours ago, and that I would do well to imitate him.

"It will only be for a short while, Wolfgang," Bach explained, as always mild-mannered. "And I will come by when I return and make sure you are safely sleeping with the angels."

But when he did return, my friend Christel, past midnight, he went straight to his own room, he forgot his promise to me.

"Thank God, dear Abel," he said in German, laughing, "that, thanks to your persuasion, Gainsborough did not play the bassoon. If he had dared to pipe half a tune I would have been obliged to beat him over the head with it, mark my words."

Abel guffawed back. "Then he would not have painted your portrait. So if you wish your image to endure for posterity, that is the price you pay, your ears must pay!"

"And would have paid even more if Dr. Johnson had ever learned, as he so devoutly wishes, to play the fiddle!"

"Yes, yes. Though he says that of all noises, music is the least disagreeable, he would retract that opinion if he had to listen to his own self! Fortunately for him, he is half deaf already!"

They were overcome with hilarity at this exchange, and Clementina and Polly joined in and this time they spoke in English, so I could not understand what they were saying, only that I was excluded from their gaiety.

I waited for the footsteps of my friend, but the footsteps did not come, there would not be a chance to deliver Jack Taylor's message tonight.

What did come were other sounds, floating from nearby rooms, disputing the sounds that had been filling my head as I tossed and turned sleeplessly, overpowering the fond memories of the dinner and the award and my playing Johann Sebastian Bach with his youngest son, night sounds of a different nature.

The loud voice of Abel, the gentler one of Christel, the sighs of Polly, the gasps of Clementina. One man like a cello, the other like a violin, one woman's voice rising like a clarinet, the other's swooning like an oboe, and no piano played by young Mozart, no notes played by me and added to that quartet longing for an eternity I could understand but not the real origin of those sounds, that was a mystery.

Though I would have dearly wanted one of them, one of the four, to visit me and tuck me in, kiss me on the nose, though I was pining for the presence of some adult seraph to dispel my anxieties, I knew better than to slip out of bed and blunder into the bedrooms of adults late at night. I had heard a similar sweet and disturbing outcry emanating furtively from my Papa and my Maman on our travels, sighs and cries and grunts and rustling of sheets and ruffling of pillows and creaking of boards. Nannerl had admonished me not to explore the source of such a quiet commotion, she had not deigned to explain why, though she had told me how she had angered my parents by suddenly interrupting their delights one night.

Twelve years later, for the first time but not the last one, I would produce those noises myself, I would occasion my little cousin Bäsle to bring them to life for me. I would catch up with my mentor Bach, I would no longer be banished to a distant bed, I would no longer be a distant ear listening from afar.

But then, on that threshold of a night, that crossroads in my life, it was loneliness that swamped my senses. Everywhere, everybody else was accompanied. Only I was by myself, in the dark.

Softly, I began to cry. So softly, I could not hear my own sobs or the beating of the heart that had learned the rhythm of the cosmos from my mother's heart. So softly, so diffidently, that I did not realize I was falling asleep, drifting off into dreams where Jack Taylor was operating on my eyes and bringing them light so I could contemplate his buttons and find out where they were sold, and then I was reading his father's titles of nobility, all of this jumbled together with visions of a woman serving two men from a barrel of wine. Suddenly, the Chevalier was there, in my dreams. It must have been him, a tall, handsome, sturdy man. "To be blind is to be dead among the living," he hissed at me as he took out the tools of his trade and laid them on a table next to his certificates and degrees. "To be always in one continued night. To be deprived from all sweets of the light. To be blind is, of all states, the most lamented. Do you wish for me to leave you in the dark forever? Will you do my son's bidding, as you have sworn you will?"

I answered yes in the dream and reiterated that yes when I awoke the next morning, after a night of similar images bobbing in and out of my mind, Jack Taylor and his father helping me through the night, getting me through the night, depositing me on the other side of the night and, finally, dawn.

I awoke and God had not transported me away and it was time to keep my promise, test the mettle of my valor.

I could choose to betray my mentor's confidence in me or I could choose to betray myself.

The moment arose immediately after breakfast.

"Taylor? Taylor? Again? Yet again?"

His rage was, thankfully, directed not toward me but toward the interlopers, as he called them.

I had barely been able to explain Jack Taylor's full message. Only that I had met him and his son, that they seemed worthy people, that they begged him to receive the Chevalier so—

That was when he erupted like a volcano.

"First the old charlatan and now his son! Using a child like you to approach me! What effrontery! What a family of brigands, a gang of rogues, a lineage of scoundrels and quacks!"

I was not giving up this easily.

"But, dear sir, most dear Maestro, what have they done to you to merit such harsh words?"

He looked at me with gentleness.

"Oh, my boy, my young, young boy, so unversed in the evils of the world. Do you remember the pieces by my father that we played last night after dinner?"

How could I forget? How could I ever forget?

Once Clementina had sung my aria and I had, at the pianoforte, performed four hands with my mentor one of his compositions and then gone on to play one of my own pieces for the fashionable assembly, once I had received plaudits and, of course, the snuffbox—it was all inlaid with gold, it was, it was!—once our guests seemed ready to move on to the Angelos' residence to continue their perpetual festivities, the London Bach lifted an admonitory hand that would not admit denial.

"You asked, Milord, to listen to some trifle from my father, Johann Sebastian Bach, and I suggested that our young prodigy might satisfy your curiosity. Well, here are two pieces. Come, Wolfgang, let us see how you fare with these counterpoint exercises my father left behind for our pleasure and puzzlement."

He set before me a page with the title *Art of the Fugue, Contrapunctus IV.*

To say it was divine would not be insulting to God.

It soothingly pursued its own melody into some semblance of eternity, each note stepping on the next transparency, escaping the previous chord and then being surpassed by it, like stars wishing to be a sun so that the sun itself could sweetly swallow them and the moon as well, a chain of quiet fire burning with a light so tender and bright that it overwhelmed us all.

When I was done, there was silence, a silence like there must have been before God Himself decided to create all that exists, a silence to which we all must return, but comforted at least, those who heard that fugue, that there had to be somewhere else we were going, that meanwhile here was this consolation, this defiance of death.

They knew, Lord Thanet and his wife, they now knew, as did I, who Johann Sebastian Bach was.

And then his son placed before me a composition, *Contrapunctus XIV* this one, this one even more drastically beautiful, another fugue that went on and on in search of a sound and a sight superior even to what we had just heard, what I had just played, it went on and on and I did not want it to end ever, I wanted to keep chasing that vision beyond every night of existence, I wanted and my audience wanted to never cease this quest, for as long as we were on this journey we were as immortal souls, we touched that intimation of eternity in the flower and the shadow, we wanted to never be deprived of more and more and more.

And then I stopped.

I turned the page to connect with that more and evermore and...

There was nothing there.

This time the silence was stunned and wretched and disconsolate.

"It is unfinished," whispered Johann Christian Bach. "My father died before he could finish it."

And now, the next morning, he was asking if I remembered that piece and the one that went before, those two fugues.

"Yes," I said. "I shall never forget them in my life."

"It is because of this Taylor, calling himself Chevalier, when he should dub himself cheval, it is because of this quack and defiler of God's gifts that my father never completed that fugue."

"What did Taylor do?"

"He killed my father. First blinded him, then killed him."

I was aghast. The Chevalier? A murderer? His son, an accomplice? It could not be. Someone else must have committed that terrible deed. I had to go forth, as my aria demanded, *Va, del furor portate*, go forth, but I would do so without fury, in order to reveal the real traitor in this affair. A deception, there had to be some sort of deception here, and if I was really the hero of this story, I was the one destined to bravely disclose it.

Gritting my teeth, I made the mistake of confusing valor with foolishness, and expressed my reservations out loud: "Begging your forgiveness, dear sir, but surely there is some sort of misunderstanding."

My mentor was a peaceful man, a serene man, of cheerful disposition and exceeding good nature. But now he launched into a rant, akin to the fugue I had played last night, but a diabolical one, one layer of bile and spite after another, over and into and over into another word, on and on, each word chasing the next one, overtaking it, devouring it, spitting it out, hunting down the one about to appear before it could be formulated, all confusion and chaos.

I cowered, recalling similar spells that battered my father, placating my fear with the knowledge that they never went on forever. But this one seemed to defy that prediction, continuing unabated for more minutes than I could count. Until my mild mentor, finally realizing how he was petrifying me, began to control his ill-tempered diatribe. As his rage began spending itself, I gathered my wits about me and asked him to allow me to understand what had transpired to thus enrage him, to please take me through the dreadful sequence of events that had led to his father's demise at the hands of the Chevalier, step by step, please, in a calm and chronological and systematic way, as if to remind him that I was presumably the child here and he the mature adult.

The Chevalier had arrived in Leipzig with ostentatious fanfare, Christian said, toward the end of March 1750, part of a grand tour of every duchy and princedom where the German tongue was spoken. He gave several lectures at the

concert hall that were so well attended and caused such awe
and admiration among the scholars and high personages
that Johann Sebastian Bach was persuaded to allow the
Oculist to perform his famous eye surgery.

"My father's vision had been declining for years"—
Christian now spoke quietly, without a trace of his previous
vehemence, his anger seemingly purged—"but, of late, Father Bach's sight started to weaken to the point that he was
increasingly unable to provide lessons, conduct the choir and
the orchestra, or write his own letters. For the latter, he used
an assistant, Johann Adam Franck, to whom he also dictated
from time to time some compositions, though on some occasions, I am proud to say, he relied on my services, even if
I was barely more than fourteen. But my father was a robust
man and there was no sign, other than the darkening cloud
in his eyes, that anything was wrong with him. By the time,
however, that this impostor Taylor sailed into town, the pain
in his eyes had become unbearable."

The Chevalier had operated on Johann Sebastian Bach
on the last day of March of that year—with a miraculous
result. In the first days of April, the bandages had been lifted
like a curtain, and, lo and behold, Christian's father had
recovered his vision. The family and indeed the whole city
celebrated—prematurely, it turned out, as a few hours later
the pain returned, accompanied this time by total darkness.
"My father did not seem desperate," explained Christian,
"giving the impression that he took this misfortune in his
stride. After a day of prayer, fasting, and meditation, he

called for the Oculist. Taylor must have been busy destroy-
ing other people's eyes, because he did not straightaway
make an appearance. When he deigned to visit our quarters,
Father Bach required family, friends, and pupils to leave him
alone with the peripatetic doctor. We complied. What they
spoke about in private during several hours we never found
out, but when Taylor left the room he announced that two
days hence, on April eighth, before leaving Leipzig on his
way to again attend our monarch Frederick of Prussia, he
would perform a second operation, and this one, he insisted,
would offer the patient everything he had been hoping for.
Those were his exact words, the bastard. As if he enjoyed
mocking us, as if he didn't know that later, on a morning like
this one, Wolfgang, I would recall those words: *everything the
patient had been hoping for.*"

Christian closed his eyes as if conjuring up a scene in
front of him.

He had been present, he said, during the operation.

Taylor laid out his utensils on a piece of cloth next to
Johann Sebastian's bed. His delicate and firm hands chose
to start with a tiny instrument made all of gold, fashioned
like a file at its extremities. *It may look like a thorn and prick like
a thorn,* the Oculist stated, *but its effect is such that your esteemed
father will soon contemplate every color of the rose, that emblem of God.*
He passed his pestilent device slowly along the conjuncti-
val sac. "I know this term," Christian clarified, "because
the charlatan talked nonstop during the whole episode, as
if he were in a theater, a prima donna in an opera, a high

priest officiating Mass. He drained the eye of some brackish
liquid, depressing the opaque material, he said, below the
level of the pupil. My father did not protest, though it must
have been excruciating indeed, as the quack was piercing
the cornea, gouging something from inside the eye itself,
cutting and slicing, now deploying a larger implement, and
all the while elegantly explaining the ophthalmology of it
all—oh, his German was excellent, only in his knowledge of
languages was he not fraudulent. *Now to the nervous filament*,
he said. He repeated the same series of devilish interven-
tions in the other eye. I could not help it, I was mesmerized
by his manual dexterity, the way his fingers fascinated the
air, as if playing a harp. *Good-bye, good-bye, damned cataracts*, he
addressed these scars as if on friendly terms with them. My
father still did not cry out. Taylor then applied a cold, wet
compress to both sockets, secured them with two bandages
of black taffeta that he drew from his pocket. I noticed they
were dirty, perhaps covered with mucus, perhaps with some
other white substance. *Special powders*, he elucidated when he
saw me look askance. *There*, he concluded jubilantly, *the deed
is done. Tomorrow all will be as he has demanded. Take the bandages
off tomorrow, I say, and ask him if he is satisfied.* Taylor put away
his torture instruments, packed them neatly into his bag.
He made one final recommendation, that the Kapellmeister should be bled. *His humors have been disturbed and must be
aligned. A knife is better than leeches, remember that. I would perform
it myself but no longer dispose of the time*, he said, *your monarch
awaits me four days hence in Berlin, call a barber and have the man*

do the bloodletting. Taylor then presented his exorbitant bill to my mother, was promptly paid, and was gone. It would be the last time I saw him."

The next day, the bandages had been removed and Johann Sebastian Bach was completely blind.

"And your father's reaction?"

"*We do not lose heart.* That's what he said. Corinthians."

A log suddenly rolled from the fireplace, lifting some sparks. Christian rose to poke it back into place. Flames danced wildly up, illuminating his face. He turned to me.

"He drew comfort from Two Corinthians, those verses. *Though outward man may perish, yet inner man is being renewed.* And added: *For things which are seen are temporary, but the things which are not seen are eternal.* He was a saintly man."

Saintly, Sebastian Bach might well be, but from that second operation on, his health began to deteriorate, his whole body falling into the most dreadful disarray. Only once, ten days before his demise, on July 28, 1750—"almost in the very middle of the century," noted Christian—did Father Bach recuperate his sight. Just for a few hours. *Yes, yes,* Johann Sebastian exclaimed and went to the window and looked out onto the limpid expanse of the sky that day over Leipzig, it was hot and blue and filled with birds. He looked out onto the pale city where Christian had been born and said again, *Yes, yes, it must be so*—and then closed his eyes and was paralyzed by a stroke and consumed by a raging fever.

And yet still creative.

It was after that ghastly operation on April 8 that the elder Bach had composed the two pieces I had played last night for Lord Thanet at my mentor's instigation, one of them forever unfinished. Father Bach had also fiddled with an organ chorale and did some work, Christian said, on an addition to his Mass in B Minor: *Et Incarnatus Est*, but "we were unable to find the score, as it mysteriously disappeared."

There was no doubt in the mind of all attending physicians, including the eminent Professor Samuel Theodor Quellmatz, head of the Leipzig Faculty of Medicine, that the Kapellmeister's decline and death were due to the operation inflicted by the Chevalier, this notorious and arrogant man who, the Herr Professor stated, "spread darkness rather than light" wherever he went.

"And your father did not curse the Chevalier, not once, not one word of reproach or regret?"

"He was not a resentful man. And more urgent matters weighed on his mind. He had to meet his Maker, the God he had served since he was a child as old as you are now, when, at the age of nine, he lost first his mother and then his father. At least I had the luck to count on his protection and instruction till I was fourteen, almost fifteen. But it was the end of my life as I knew it then. I was forced to leave home, to seek shelter elsewhere, and never return."

My friend paused and, again, grief seemed to overwhelm him. For a while, he did not speak. He stared into space, some spot on the ceiling, some zone within, finally pursed his lips and nodded.

"Of course, my loss is nothing compared to what the world lost, what music lost, the cantatas that will never be composed, the sonatas he still had inside him, the fugue he left unfinished. And now this charlatan pretends to…"

Again he stopped, looked at me as if realizing it was a child to whom he had been talking all this while.

"I am sorry, young Wolfgang. Please forgive the diatribe unleashed upon your ears, as well as this narrative of human perversity that you could well do without. I can only hope that nonetheless it serves a purpose. You are now of an age, as was my father when he suffered the disappearance of both parents and had to venture into a hostile world, where you must begin to distinguish between what people say and what they do. And now, enough, I promised your own father, may he live to a ripe old age, to return you early so you could go to Mass. He and your mother must be worried."

"And my sister. She will not get better unless her brother is by her side. I am composing a violin sonata to cheer her up. We will play it together when her throat clears."

"Yes, yes, of course, your sister. Only natural you should be—"

"I have never been separated from her and never will," I exclaimed. "We will live in our own Black Kingdom forever, and even die the same day. That way I'll never be lonely again."

The London Bach looked again toward the fire, almost rose once more to revive the embers, thought better of it.

"*Forever* is a dangerous word, Wolfgang," he said, solemnly. "We use it at our peril. Nothing is forever except death. Not sisters. Not brothers. Not home, the paradise to which we never can return." Again, a fog crossed his face, passed, then revived and settled there. "You must forgive my dark mood. I do not like to recall the circumstances of my father's passing from this world or the man who defiled him. And it is time to call for my carriage and transport you to the caring embrace of your parents."

In spite of these words, he did not move.

"Though not yet, am I right? You have something else to add about the conversation you had with the Chevalier's son? Deliver it, come, the whole thing, let's finish this infernal affair once and for all."

He was right. I had not transmitted Jack Taylor's remarks about Queen Charlotte. I had held them back when he had erupted with such fury and would not have now filled in that part of the story if I had not seen him subside into his usual benevolent self, a man who saw only my angelic nature, who did not wish to profit from my exploits or my fame, someone who simply loved me for myself.

And so I transmitted Jack Taylor's request that he tell Her Majesty the truth, the truth about what really happened between the two fathers.

This time my friend did not explode, did not make me fear for his sanity and mine. He merely smiled bitterly, then frowned, then smiled again, more of a grin this time, a vindication of some sort.

"So that's what all this is about! Praise God, Jack Taylor has been refused the license of Oculist to the King! Our

good and mighty sovereign, George the Third, has listened
to his wife, who has with discretion informed His Majesty
that the elder Taylor is a treacherous quack. This has reflected badly upon the son, who now seeks me out as *Maître
de Musique* to the Queen, that I may intervene. The truth?
The truth is that I had only mentioned my father's blindness
to Her Majesty in passing, not wishing to burden her with
my woes, how the greatest musician of his time was thrust
into darkness, unable to compose for the glory of God and
His creatures. The truth? I did not tell her the real truth,
only a snippet of it. The truth, the truth—he wants me to
tell her the truth. That I will. You are sure to see him again.
Men of his ilk never give up, they will try to corrupt everything around them. So when he next approaches you, when
he—why, I wager he is out in the street now, with his dreadful son. Come, let us look through the window."

Sure enough. There, on the southwest corner of the
square, standing in front of a carriage, its two horses stomp-
ing in the cold, there was Dr. Jack Taylor with his uneven
teeth chattering, next to his ten-year-old boy, who was darting back and forth as if possessed, no, not possessed, that
child, my counterpart, was holding back a need to piss, holding it in, how long had the two of them been there, waiting?

"Go to him, child. Let us not be vindictive. The horses
and children do not deserve to suffer in this weather due
to the ambitions of foolish jobseekers. He awaits a reply,
and I, unlike his father, am not a cruel man. Tell him I will
minutely inform the Queen about the truth. I will repeat,

though in a more moderate and respectful tone, the story I have today revealed to you. I will make sure that the son of such a villain never gets a chance to blind the King, as he did my father. Go, give him my response."

I did not move.

This time, he was the one keeping something back.

How could I tell this, being so ingenuous and, as my father did not cease to repeat, easily deceived at that tender age, that I was too trusting with strangers, not caring if someone was a king or a cook, so much did I wish for caresses and affection and adoration from all. That might be so, but then, what devil inside me had tutored me, how could I be reading below the surface of Johann Christian Bach, so much older and experienced than me, from what deep instinct did I guess that something was missing from his response, perhaps missing from the tale he had recounted just now? As if we were a musical score that had notes that still need to be added, his version of the events as unfinished as his father's final fugue.

It was that intuition—that there was more mystery to this affair than the inexplicable disappearance of the *Et Incarnatus Est*—that some part of the truth he claimed to be defending was being hidden, it was this ability of mine, unrecognizable to my father, that encouraged me to deliver Jack Taylor's final, enigmatic message.

"Handel," I said.

"What?"

"Taylor said to tell you, if all else failed, that Handel held the key."

"He said that? Exactly that?"

I thought a bit. Shook my head. "No, sir. He said Handel knew the truth. That his father keeps muttering that Handel knew the truth, and that I was to make you aware of this circumstance."

"Handel?"

My friend's shoulders slumped. He sat himself down, as if exhausted. For a while he remained there, the only sound his fingers tapping against the armchair next to the window.

"What should I tell him, then?"

Johann Christian Bach nodded, as if to himself, as if he had been debating a point with some inner region of his being and was now convinced of…what? His response startled me. "I am not, I repeat, a cruel man. Tell that man down there I will not see him. Nor the charlatan of his father. Nor any Taylors. Ever. But this I will do, this you can report back to him. Out of deference for you and your innocence, out of regard for your judgment about this Jack Taylor's good faith, I will henceforth abstain from attacking the Chevalier in private or in public…"

"Oh, he will be most content with this response, he will—"

"…unless drastically provoked, unless I am given cause. In that case, I will express my opinions with renewed and fierce vigor, I will reveal all. Make sure he understands that we have a pact and that I am not the one who intends to break this truce. And make sure he also understands that he owes this boon to your affable intervention."

I did his bidding.

Down in the frozen street, Jack Taylor listened attentively to my mentor's offer—I was brief, I did not inform
him at any length about his father's role in the death of Johann Sebastian Bach—and nodded his head without even
a hint of being surprised. "You see, young John," he said,
addressing his son, "it is as I feared. Well, we have done our
best. Tell Maestro Bach that I appreciate his offer. I will no
longer pursue the post of Oculist to George the Third nor
the honor of such an assignment. But tell him also that the
truth has not yet been told. The truth will out, tell him, like
an excrescence is squeezed from an infected eye. I do not
myself know that truth, but someday, young sir, I will come
to you with it and you will then transmit it to Johann Christian Bach. On that day, near or far away, I beseech you that
you open your heart to me then as you have opened it now,
may you be forever blessed. Do you promise to listen to me
that day?"

I made the promise, what else could I do?

I did not know that it would be thirteen years before I
again saw Jack Taylor.

I did not know that when he finally did come to me, my
mother would be dying.

Part Two

PARIS

Paris, June 18, 1778.

Andante

I was slowly, deliciously, guiltily, licking an ice at the Palais-Royal after my triumphal debut at the Concert Spirituel when I next saw Jack Taylor.

Was I glad that he and his smile came back into my life at that precise instant in my existence?

Never had I been more in need of a friendly face from the past. Except for the taste of that heavenly ice soothing my throat, lick lick, on that torrid Thursday evening, nothing else was going well. My Paris sojourn—three months had passed, could it be, since Maman and I had arrived here?—had turned into a disaster.

But that was not what I was trying to concentrate on in the minutes before I remarked Jack Taylor hovering, as

usual, at the margins of the crowd surrounding me, wanting
and not wanting to call attention to himself, his gaunt body,
his crooked teeth.

Better to count my measly blessings with each slip of
cool sweetness flavoring my tongue. Starting with the obvious: lick lick, I was not paying for this ice, thank our Mother
of Mercy it had been bought as a present by a Mademoiselle whose name I never knew or forgot or didn't care to
remember, utterly unknown to me but not me to her, cooing
at me about my new symphony. Lick lick, it had gone well,
she had been impressed, she said as she fluttered her fan at
her ample bosom and my florid face, chasing the heat away,
étonnée, she insisted, at the heroic beat of the Allegro Assai,
flourishes and trumpets and a jubilant ride—and then, licking away, she and the rest of the audience were really transfixed when I introduced something different in the middle
of that first movement, a delightful refuge from the previous
dramatic storm, the rain held at bay, if only for an interlude,
and haven and heaven and lick lick lick when I returned to
that melody with a victorious fanfare at the end of the Allegro, they burst into applause and unparalleled cries of "Da
capo" went up. And then the Andante gave them something
deeper and perhaps more disturbing to dwell on, lick on,
charmant, my ice-lady-benefactress stressed without understanding what I was doing, no wonder Legros—oh, this di-
rector of the Concert Spirituel is such a bore—did not favor
it, so just one lick here. But back to my tasting splendor: in
the third movement, another Allegro, I thrust upon these

Parisians what they had never heard before in this city, oh
how they and I are licking it all up! Instead of launching
the final movement with all the instruments, as is custom-
ary, I began with two very gentle violins, and the spectators
started whispering *Hush, hush,* like a lenient breeze coursing
through them, and then I stirred and surprised them with
the forte of the full orchestra and they began to clap—in the
middle of my piece, lick lick lick lick! May they continue to
clap, may this ice creaming my tongue never end either, may
this stay in Paris give me the prosperity and acclaim—and a
post! a permanent post!—that I crave and require for myself
and the family and...perhaps someone else, for a girl with
a heavenly voice and other attributes just as lively, oh, if she
could see me now, she would say yes to me, yes, you will
triumph just as your symphony has.

But the symphony had now ended. The ice was dimin-
ishing, the concert over, Mademoiselle did not seem disposed to treat me to another one, so glad I don't have to
remember her name.

And I was left to face the reality, under that savage setting sun that would melt any hope of redress, that I could
not afford such a tasty luxury myself. I owed 350 gulden to
Baron von Grimm, no matter how much the audience savored the smoothness of my music, and more funds from the
Baron would not be forthcoming unless I mended my ways
and obeyed his instructions, listened patiently to his scold-
ing and affronts. Last night I had gambled away at cards the
last money left in my last pocket. Gambled away the twenty

louis d'or loaned to me by M le Duc de Guines when I went to teach composition to his untalented daughter, funds I require, I told him, so I can start to repay von Grimm—oh, von Grimm was so welcoming to me when I was a child here in Paris and is now so nasty, I doubt I will ever again be able to coax another hundred from his stingy fist. To make matters worse, I owed much more, close to 900 gulden, to my own father, who had just refused to authorize me to draw one more pfennig from the account that he established in my name. No licking the juice oozing from a nice roast or perfectly fried eggs or the toss of oil in a salad, no salt, no sugar, no milk, no more credit with tradespeople—and honor would soon vanish as well if the reprehensible news of my debts were to get out.

No help from anyone, no help, unless, unless—well, there was Jack Taylor.

My father had told me, before Maman and I had left Salzburg for Mannheim almost a year ago, he had warned me to confide in no one until I had proof of their sincerity. Good advice for Paris, bursting with jealous enemies out to destroy me. But Jack Taylor, yes, I felt I could trust. He had not bothered me again, had behaved like a gentleman, seemed to have kept his part of the pact of peace I had negotiated when I was a boy in London. I was pallidly aware that my trust in him here in Paris might derive from the fact that he came to me from many yesterdays ago, a reminder of a time when I was recognized as a prodigy of Nature whose brilliant future nobody dared doubt. And now

that the future had arrived with its ugly impoverished vis-
age, the mere presence of the Chevalier's son was comforting, he might be of assistance in my time of sudden penury.
Though, watch out, be alert, he must be desiring something
from me yet again—there could be no other reason for his
obsequious inclination of the head, his eyes above the apolo-
getic crooked teeth beaming at me—but at least his presence
anchored me to a glorious past, spurred me to believe in the
glorious future that might still perhaps materialize, oh, if
only enough people had faith in my talents, a faith that Jack
Taylor, having effusively praised my genius thirteen years
ago, might still harbor.

A while passed, nonetheless, before Jack and I spoke to
each other.

I was waiting for someone else to step forward and buy
me an ice, and he was waiting for the crowd of ephemeral
devotees to disperse. His wish came true before mine did.

I was alone under the arches of the Palais-Royal, I was
alone as the sun started to say good-bye to the nearby waters
of the Seine, when he finally approached me.

His son was not with him.

This time he addressed me in French. His was better
than mine, with not a discernible accent.

"Again, good sir, I intrude on you and beg your indulgence and benevolence."

"There is no reason to beg, Mr. Taylor."

"Alas, it concerns once more your mentor, the honorable Johann Christian Bach. He is now in Paris, as you well

know, and I would indeed beg for you to intercede so that we may finally meet—as you promised when last I saw you on a day slightly colder than this one."

This is not what I had expected. I had been awaiting the London Bach's arrival in Paris with joy, something to really look forward to among much dismal news, that my friend Christel would take me under his wing. Not only under his wing: take me to the theater and the opera, which I could ill afford to attend by myself. And advise me as to how one must avoid the pack of mediocrities filling every post, musical and otherwise. He'd side with me against so much pressure, from my father, from Baron von Grimm, from Madame d'Épinay—oh, she might be a friend of Voltaire and Rousseau, but how wearisome her insistence that I bow to what she called *les circonstances*, all of them conspiring, determined to make me accept the position of Royal Organist at the Court—what, would they imprison a young man of such genius in faraway, dreary, pompous Versailles for six months, tied to an organ of dubious quality, unable to give lessons or receive commissions, cut off from the eminent musicians visiting Paris? For what? For a pittance? And Johann Christian Bach might well advance my plans to move to England, where I was really appreciated, where I could set myself up in ways that would solve all the problems of the family and perhaps a little someone else if she was willing. And now, from that very England, trouble in the figure of Jack Taylor, trouble rather than the succor I yearned for.

No, no, it was better not to get involved. Thirteen years ago, my childhood innocence could excuse interfering in Johann Christian's affairs. But to risk my mentor's wrath now, at the plump age of twenty-two, by shepherding a sworn enemy into his presence, went against my own interests, my own need to beg Bach's indulgence and benevolence. True, I did not wish to disappoint Jack Taylor, either, who liked me so much and who, at the age of fifty-some years, still exhibited a childlike vulnerability that made my heart ache. And how well dressed he was, he must have known some success during this long interval!

Fortunately, destiny had made it easy for me to avoid the unpleasantness of having to reject Taylor in favor of Johann Christian.

Just a week earlier, Carl Friedrich Abel, passing through Paris, had reported that Bach's visit to France had been delayed. Noting my dejection at this news—though there were more serious reasons for the melancholy welling up inside me—he had insisted that I needed cheering up and had taken me on a whirlwind tour of nocturnal Paris, taverns, billiard rooms, a gaming house near the Louvre where we both lost more than what was prudent, and, finally, his favorite brothel. "Women," he rasped as he rapped the heavy knocker on the door, "if you do not know where the women moan and sleep in any city, it is better to shun that damned place, Wolfgang. I have made the intimate acquaintance of a comely breast and thigh or two in there that will make you forget that our friend Christel has not arrived yet in Paris.

He can teach you about violins and horns, but he wouldn't have brought you to this sacred temple, doesn't even know this house of mirth exists. Aren't you lucky I came along instead?" I didn't tell him no, that I would rather have my very own Bach in Paris, but I did demur to follow him into the gaudy cavern of the bordello. Watching him disappear into the arms and wide bosom of a large red-haired prostitute made me feel all the more eager for the company of Johann Christian and any sober advice he might provide as to my future.

My past sorrow at the postponement of Bach's arrival in the French capital was now somewhat mitigated. At least I would not need to honor the childish promise of assistance I had given to Jack Taylor.

"What I know, sir," I said to him, "is that Baron Bach is expected here in a month's time or more, and is presently in London, from where, it is my guess, you have just arrived? Perhaps you might better seek him there?"

Taylor's distress was evident.

"What? In London? He's in London, you say, and not here, not in Paris, as they—oh, that was not a noble thing to do, to trick me thus. My informants—oh, a conspiracy they've indulged in at my expense, oh, a pox upon their house, that they should make me believe he had left when all the while he must have been laughing behind the door when his footman gave me the news. But no, that is too cruel, I do not and will not and cannot believe such villainy of the good Queen's *Maître de Musique*, he would not go so far as to send me on a fool's errand and dispense such an outlay of funds I can ill afford, that would have better gone toward treating the poor and the miserable and the infirm at Hatton Gardens. It must be some misunderstanding. All those who confirmed his trip must have implied he was planning to come here, and not that he had already departed. Not realizing that I am compelled, compelled by the living and the dead to speak to him, get this over with once and for all."

I was about to ask him what had gone wrong, how was it that the truce of these thirteen years so successfully plotted had so abruptly been broken, but—who knew how long the answer might take or where it would lead. I had been away from home for far too long that day, and there were several stops on my scattered and twisted route back to rue du Gros Chenet. And tomorrow promised to be busier still. I began to regret the time lost on the ice, no matter how delicious and deserved and gratis it had been, amid the nagging suspicion that perhaps I had accepted that flavorful frozen gift because I was seeking, unawares, to distract myself precisely from the urgent command to return to the residence where Maman awaited me. Was that the origin of the temptation to tarry with Jack Taylor and learn details of his falling-out with Johann Christian Bach, just another way of avoiding the scene that awaited me in my quarters?

Better, in any case, to leave explanations for another occasion, if such a morrow were ever to dawn, if Jack Taylor did not decide to immediately depart to London to confront his father's adversary.

I mumbled an inane excuse, told him I was sorry he had gone to all that bother, lamented I could do no more for him—and bid him adieu.

He would have none of it.

"Allow me, then, to accompany you, Monsieur Mozart. I declare that I have no other imperative business."

"You will miss your coach back to London."

That is when he avowed, quite matter-of-factly, that he did not mean to leave Paris until Herr Bach arrived. My intervention all those years ago had proved to be prodigious, after months of fruitless endeavors, and he saw no reason to change a tactic that had so brilliantly worked in the past.

Would he then stalk and hassle me for the next month or so? Would he be my shadow as I struggled with more ominous shadows that beleaguered me without mercy? Would he ruin and corrode my relationship with my mentor? And he was obviously as penurious as I was, could offer little or no benefaction in return for my help.

I was determined to be firm.

"Let me insist, Dr. Taylor," I said, "that there is nothing I can do for you. I bid you farewell and good luck."

I bowed ceremoniously and set out under the arches of the Palais-Royal, the late-afternoon sun burning my back.

He walked with me, or rather, nearby, on the elaborate garden path that ran parallel to the darker passageway that I was traversing, all the while never ceasing to talk, partly to me, mostly as if musing to himself, spelling out with a tinge of bewilderment how it was that he and his beseeching eyes found themselves traipsing through Paris with a twenty-two-year-old musician from Salzburg.

And I could not help but eavesdrop. Not only because I was curious as to the outcome of something that had started that faraway night, the fascinating culmination of the as-yet-unfinished sonata of his existence. But also because he was not the only one necessitating assistance, not the only one alone and stranded in a foreign land. Perhaps giving him solace and refuge was the best way of finding some myself, though I quickly rejected the idea—you must cease, I heard my father's voice, being so kindhearted—and picked up the pace of my strides. He had, however, longer legs, and seemed, for such a thin man, to be in excellent physical shape, probably did not devote his nights to gambling and playing billiards.

"You must be wondering, dear Master Mozart, why this urgency, so unforeseen? Especially as you surely know that my father, the Chevalier, died six years ago—in this very city."

I felt sorry for this news, but preferred not to reestablish a conversation by offering a belated condolence. I pressed on, nodding in his direction, to indicate that I understood what the loss of a father meant, especially far from home.

"Perhaps that is a sign from heaven, that I have not been sent mistakenly, after all, here to Paris—that it should be in the city where he expired that I must now set right his reputation. That is why Johann Christian Bach is instructed by God and His sweet son Jesus to come to my encounter."

Though I had resolved not to speak and certainly not to mention the name of Bach, this suggestion of divine intervention—of which I myself had dire need—on Corpus Christi, of all dates, seemed so outrageous for such a frivolous enterprise—a meeting between rivals!—that I interjected a remark:

"I beg your pardon, dear sir, but he does not come to see you but to audition singers for his opera, you know, *Amadis de Gaule*, it's called, you know, based on that book of chivalry, a chivalry we must all learn from, but what I meant to explain is that he intends to stay several weeks to continue composing it, so yes, he will in effect be here, but I doubt in a better mood to receive you than in London. The blazing heat here will not, I believe, have melted what was already frozen back then—and I do not refer only to the weather, sir."

"It is a sign, I say, and when he arrives, you will confirm that it was destiny that made this transpire. But I stray from my story. How is it that all these years after my dear father departed this world I suddenly sought to speak to Herr Bach? It is a chain of iniquity that brings me here, so maybe you are right, maybe it is Satan who is interfering and not God. But bear with me and you will hear why and how and wherefore and when. Less than a month ago, my patron, the Duke of Ancaster, remarked one day to a friend that I had cured a violent inflammation in his eyes, the Duke's, I mean. This friend, Topham Beauclerk, who is regarded as an ill-tempered and filthy man, though he be the great grandson of King Charles the Second, recalled that this oculist Jack

Taylor so highly recommended was the son of the Chevalier, whose memoir was dedicated to Garrick. So this fop Beau-clerk asked Garrick, that great actor, for a copy and read the contents to see if there was anything nasty to be discovered there. He chanced upon a passage in which my father mentioned having cured the teacher of the great Handel, Johann Sebastian Bach, at the age of eighty-eight years—and this dreadful Beauclerk proceeded to call upon Johann Christian Bach to ascertain the truth—"

This flurry of gossip was deadly dull to me. There is nothing worse in this world than being bored—it is then that you feel time slipping away, wasting away—and I was in no mood for anything to waste away, let alone time, of which I had not much that evening, so I asked him, with non-Parisian impoliteness, to cut the matter short, to come to the point.

He looked surprised. Perhaps he thought he was still dealing with a child of nine. He hurried his pace and his tongue: "Your mentor Johann Christian informed this blackguard Beauclerk that this was the first time he had heard of this foolishness and that this changed everything, everything."

At this word, I perked up my ears. Everything had changed? Was this the origin of the truce having come to an end? And what did it portend for me?

Maybe Jack noted a shift in my attention, because he quickly persisted in his intricate tale: "My father, Johann Christian shouted according to my sources, died at age sixty-five, and repeated the number over several times, sixty-five, sixty-five, and was most certainly not Handel's teacher, had not even met him, and that the Devil could take that scoundrel, the Chevalier, if he had not already done so. I know of this outburst because it was duly reported to Dr. Samuel Johnson at dinner a few nights later by Beauclerk. Dr. Johnson had responded—oh, that such words should pour forth from the man who created the most sublime dictionary of the English language, from the mouth of the man who is responsible for that great periodical, the *Rambler*, oh—well he rambled, Johnson did, he quipped that this Taylor, meaning my father, was an instance of how far impudence could carry ignorance—an assertion he probably repeated to many others, but particularly to Garrick, to whom the memoir was dedicated. And Garrick came running to me to recount the whole miserable string of events."

I halted. We had arrived at the entrance to St. Eustache, my first destination. I stepped aside to allow the last of the members of the congregation to leave. I could see the procession heading toward the Pont Neuf and the Seine, holding up the Eucharist. Better: nobody would be inside. Jack Taylor did not give me the chance, however, to explain that I would now leave him in order to visit the church. Alone. He took my stop as a sign that I had repented of my previous discourtesy and was disposed to heed every last detail of his endless tale of Ancaster and Beauclerk and Garrick and Johnson, might they all be transported to the pit of hell, where they could bore each other forever, but not me, not me.

"You will ask why I had to journey to Paris, why not go to Dr. Johnson and force him, as a man of honor and purported wisdom, to retract his words. He would not receive me, instructed his servants to show me the door before it had even been opened, denied me all access. He is not, I declare, the great man that all praise, but a whore of Babylon, an indecent scribbler unversed in surgery. Has he ever held a man's fate in his hands, as I have? Did he consult the elder Bach, consult Handel, me, you, before casting his aspersions? My father, a murderer—that is tolerable, for any man can kill and still have honor. But impudent, ignorant! My father? My sire, who spoke more languages than Dr. Samuel Johson ever did, whose fingers were deft so he could cure blindness, whereas Johnson's fingers were useless, save to scribble inane poetry."

"Excuse me, Dr. Taylor, but I really cannot—"

"You are right, so right, to be indignant. Because it is your bargain that has been abrogated—and I have behaved, complied with my part. Even after my father died, here, in my arms, in Paris, even when he told me the truth about the elder Bach and the two operations on his eyes before his death and also about Handel, all that I did not know when I first met you, sir. The Chevalier died, I say, and revealed all, all, to me, what really happened—and in spite of this I did not approach Herr Bach, did not try to gain the position as Oculist to the King that by rights should be mine, I was content. But this cannot be tolerated. Herr Bach has declared war on me. And war it shall be until he goes to Johnson and demands that he repudiate those words, impudence, ignorance—and Bach shall do so once he hears from me the truth that he has been hiding from, because he did know, he did know about Handel, he did, he did!"

"This is the Church of St. Eustache," I said, pointedly. "Today is Corpus Christi."

"And not only that. There is worse. It is rumored that a certain Bosworth or Boswell or Bogwood is writing a journal wherein he consigns every utterance of Dr. Johnson on mutton and music and medicine—and that can only mean that the world will someday be able to peruse far and wide the malevolent Johnson's opinion about my father. Oh no, I will not allow it! It shall not be."

He kept repeating it shall not be, it shall not be, in ever-diminishing swoops, until, like his antagonist Johann Christian Bach thirteen years earlier, his rage eventually was extinguished, leaving me to ask myself, as I had with Bach himself, into what sort of mess had my good heart and loneliness led me? It was necessary, indeed critical, to establish that what was intolerable was his intrusion on my solitude, and I made this clear with an intensity that, once more, shocked Jack Taylor.

"You have accompanied me thus far at my pleasure, Dr. Taylor—and unless you calm yourself, I will immediately terminate this relationship, and you shall not count on my good offices to intercede when Johann Christian Bach comes to Paris. I am, in fact, not even sure if I am inclined to do so at all. I have troubles of my own. I have come to this sanctuary in order to pray, and, sir, if you are not composed and relaxed when I next emerge, then we shall henceforth have no more association."

"Oh, dear Mozart, you will, you must, forgive me. Would you have acted otherwise if your own sainted father were besmirched with such calumnies when you know the truth to be the opposite? But, please, sir, seek some moments with the Almighty without my irksome presence. I will await you out here and can solemnly swear that upon your return you will find me amended, smoking my pipe, which is a surefire way of edging me toward the bask of tranquility."

And indeed he lit his pipe and the odor of the tobacco pursued me into the pews, mixing with incense, turning the dim lights inside even more hazy for a moment.

I passed the tomb of Rameau, born in 1685, it said, which rang a bell of some sort, but I had no more time for that, because I then chanced, more ominously, on the remains of Susan Feilding, Countess of Denbigh. I did not want reminders of dead bodies, and certainly not of any countess, nothing that made me recall our dear Countess van Eyck, our hostess in Paris during our first visit, well and blooming one day, coughing the next one, dead and buried one week later. She had given me a pocket calendar for my eighth birthday, exquisitely printed in Liege, *so you may always love each day, know that each day is better than the day before,* and now those tantalizing hands of hers born in Salzburg like mine, like Maman's, would never caress me or anybody else

again, in one week, just one week she— But no, I was not at
St. Eustache to dwell on such unhappy memories.

I was there because of a debt I had to pay, a debt in-
curred just yesterday, when I had attended the rehearsal of
my new symphony, the one that not an hour ago had elicited
such acclaim at the Palais-Royal. Twice, twice, the inept
musicians had scraped and scrambled through it, and did
such an abysmal job that I had almost resolved not to be
present at today's performance. Trusting, however, in God
and His eternal wisdom—and Maman's encouraging words,
Of course you must go, you must defend what is yours, even though
she could not come with me—I had trudged to the Tuileries,
mounted to the second floor of the central pavilion, swept
into the Salle des Cent Suisses, and collected applause and
then collected an ice and had even collected the distracting
Dr. Jack Taylor! I had sworn beforehand that if all went well,
I would say, I told Maman, a Paternoster of thanks—and,
well, here I was.

I sank to my knees.

As I silently mouthed those words of gratitude, it gradually dawned on me that this Our Father was being wasted on
a mere symphonic success. That had been God's pretext to
entice me into His Temple, to test my faith. *Fiat voluntas tua
sicut in caelo et in terra*, yes, that was true, I needed to accept
that His will must be done on earth, as it is in heaven, didn't
I, didn't I? Yes, His name was sanctified and His kingdom
was coming, yes, yes, *adveniat regnum tuum*, but what of this
kingdom I inhabited, the everyday blessing of life, yes, yes,

yes, *panem nostrum quotidianum da nobis hodie*, except that nobody here in this city of damnation was giving me, was giving us, our daily bread, our daily meat, our daily medicine,
our daily lodgings, yes, yes, forgive us our trespasses, above
all that, forgive me my trespasses, *dimitte nobis debita nostra*,
yes, damn it, yes, but where the fortitude to forgive those
who trespass against us, yes or no, yes or no, and temptations, what if one did not know what was a temptation and
what was an opportunity, what was a sin and what was a
glory, lead us not?, lead us not? Was it not God Himself who
had made me thus, avid of temptations and the symphony
of life and desire, was it not God who made my body, who
filled me with such divine music to His Glory and would He
now abandon me, would He, would He? Would He really
deliver us from evil?

Would He really deliver us from evil?

Amen.

Amen?

So be it?

Desperate, I turned to the Blessed Virgin, that dank,
dribbled marble statue of her, holding the child of stone,
as my mother had held me and my flesh. Did I dare ask for
her help? After such sinful misgivings? I fingered my rosary
and started my Hail Mary and only got as far as *benedictus fructus ventris tui*, and stopped. Not in Latin! Not in this
dead language that I had not suckled at my own mother's
breast—no, no, speak directly to her in German, Woferl.
Please, please, My Lady of Sorrows, lift this burden from my

shoulders. If ever you were inclined to listen to me, may this be the one occasion. If you find my music honors you, bless me back, Holy Mother, you who understand what a son feels for his mother, what a mother feels for her child.

Save her. Save Maman.

If there is one creature in the world you can save, let it be her.

There was absolute silence in the church.

And then a last ray of the sun as it bid the earth farewell hit the red eye of a vitraux at the very top of the tallest, loftiest vault of the church's inner sky, and I was bathed, the whole shrine was bathed, in a hue of pale inflamed light, something, somebody was dipping into my soul and soothing it, boding that all would be well, reminding me that endings could be as beautiful as beginnings, that birth is happening even in the dimming of the light, so be it, so be it.

A sob racked my body. I could feel, welling inside, the old need to drain myself of every last swamp of regret, weep into the deepening dusk until nothing was left and I could stand and face the world again. That was how I had always dealt with misfortune. Run to my mother, run to my father, run to my sister, run to my friends, and cry myself clean, receive absolution from them, continue as if nothing could ever again disturb my peace. But not this time. I held back even the whisper of a wail.

I held it back because Jack Taylor was lurking outside and I had compelled him to accept that I was no longer a child. I held it back because I had consented to his company for reasons I did not yet fully understand, just as perhaps he did not understand why he had been sent here, to spend an absurd, unaffordable month in Paris while he waited for his nemesis and my mentor. But he was here and so was I and I had better make the most of his cryptic appearance on this day of the Holy Sacrament, the day I had granted the world my new symphony. Sagacity told me that it was preferable to see the man as a blessing rather than a curse, a messenger rather than a disturbance. If Johann Christian Bach was a true friend, he would empathize with me, understand that I could not compose the music as I did if I did not have a heart larger than the whole world. And if he did not empathize or understand, then why foster that relationship? Merely to feed my worldly ambitions, merely because it was circumstantially advantageous, because we had once been acquainted?

And so it was that when I faltered out from that sanctuary into the twilight of Paris, I was determined to no longer reject Taylor's company, ready to accept what that night and future nights might bring.

He snuffed out his pipe and looked at me in a strange way, as if recognizing the alteration in my mood. "Where to now?" he asked.

"An apothecary, rue des Blancs-Manteaux in Le Marais," I responded, pointing in that direction and starting out across the marketplace of Les Halles, where few people were stirring anymore. "A singer friend of mine, Anton Raaff, has told me that it closes late and may have something I have been seeking in vain for several days."

He did not inquire what it was. His unruffled silence was welcome. Perhaps that ray of the setting sun had also touched him with its balm, had also worked some transformation in his spirit.

A hand was abruptly thrust into the space between us. It belonged to a little beggar boy, blind and all covered with scabs, but even so with something candid and hopeful shining from within. He could not have been more than nine years old—and, as always, the question surged, Why him? Why not me?—and my response, as always, was to give, give, give. Plumbing my pocket, I discovered a solitary sou at the very bottom, extracted it from those indigent depths, and dropped it into the begrimed palm.

"Come here, child," said Jack Taylor, in such a gentle tone that the boy obeyed. "That looks like—let me take a closer look—that seems to be, yes—" he added, examining the left and then the right eye, lifting the eyelid and peering inside it—"yes, it can be cured, this fistula lacrymalis. If you are here tomorrow at this time, boy, I can come by and with the simplest intervention relieve you of your affliction."

The lad was taken aback.

He shook his head, began to retreat, stumbling, then disappeared around the corner of a milliner's shop.

"Ah," said Jack Taylor. "Of course. If I heal him, how will he earn his keep? And even so, I will return tomorrow and the next day, I will do my best."

The heat was abating, and all Paris seemed to have poured outdoors to enjoy the street life in the evening glow.

On la rue Montorgueil, ladies strolled, arm in arm, nattering, while their husbands or lovers followed, animatedly discussing the recent death of Voltaire. Savory smells of fried liver and onion and aromatic burgundy stews which that damned atheist would never taste again rose from a dozen houses. Domestic bliss, everywhere. Children—none of them blind, none of them crippled or scarred—chased one another down narrow alleyways, playing follow-the-leader, as I had done in Salzburg with Nannerl and Maman— games we had not forgotten in our childhood travels, that I had pursued in this Vienna all those years ago with Marie Antoinette when she raced me and then covered me with kisses as compensation for my having lost. And now she was not willing to even receive me!

Jack Taylor was respectful of my somber mood, only once interposing himself when I took a turn onto la rue de St. Martin.

"That's not the way," he said. And, in response to my mystified expression: "Not the way to la rue des Blancs-Manteaux."

I defended my choice: I was taking a short detour to a music shop. "We won't be delayed by more than a few minutes," I said, apologetically, as if he were the one in a hurry to get home instead of me. "But I am impressed with how well you know your way around this city."

As we mounted the street, he explained that he had spent five years in Paris at the College du Plessis. "I was ten when my father deposited me here—to expand my horizons, he said. 'Tis useless, said he, to be an expert on the eye and not cultivate one's mind. Oh, I was not that alone," he added, noting my alarm at the thought of being left to fend at that early age without one's family, "he would come and see me once or twice a year, on his way somewhere else, and interrogate me on history and Latin and make sure my French was up to his high standards. And take me out to dinner, and spoil me and leave me a fat purse. Near la rue Saint Jacques, don't you know, there was much diversion in the Quartier Latin."

"Five years?"

"Five years. Then back to London to learn the profession at my father's feet—when his feet were there, that is. But my mother, Ann King, was an ever-loving presence, and that was sufficient. And warm memories of French maidens, former maidens, matrons, ah."

We were approaching the music shop. I could see the proprietor, sitting with his wife and some friends, drinking in the cool, contentedly disputing some point or other while they savored profiteroles and other choux pastry of choice, washed down with sips of wine. The music business must be flourishing—though not thanks to me, that was certain.

"Make sure you don't identify me by name," I warned Jack Taylor in a hushed voice, reverting to German. "He mustn't know who I am, or the bastard will never lower the price of the book I seek. It is by my very own father, a veritable treasure."

Jack Taylor nodded and grinned, glad to be part of my conspiracy.

The owner of the store, an old, bespectacled fellow with a ruddy complexion and sharp, jutting eyebrows, greeted me heartily, his mouth full of custard, though he offered us none.

"Ah, Monsieur le Professeur, you are back. More sonatas by Abel for your pupils, perhaps? Though some engravings by Salieri just came in. Exquisite. Perfect for beginners, *cher* Monsieur."

"No, I was just wondering if the price of the *Violinschule*, by that musician—I think his name was Leopold, Leopold Mozart, that's it—if the price, I say, has been reduced, as you suggested it might last month when I happened by."

"The one by Leopold Mozart? No, the price remains the same. There are only three copies left. It is quite popular, and there seems to be no reason to give it away when customers will pay handsomely. Would you give away your services for free so willingly?"

I did not wish to respond the truth to him: that I had been giving my services away for free ever since Maman and I had left Salzburg, that the rich expect music but do not wish to pay for it, that they ... Instead, I thanked him and, trying to hide my chagrin, bid the company and their profiteroles farewell—and farewell, also, to acquiring my father's book.

We set out again.

It was getting dark.

"He must have guessed who I am. He must know, the sly fox, that I want the book for my father. Papa has never seen the French translation of his lessons for the violin, though we sent him from Mannheim the Dutch version of them. A surprise I had in store for him when next I write, which must be soon, yes, it must be sooner than I would wish."

"And the price is too steep?"

"He will not lower it. And if he suspects, as I believe he already does, that I have sought this volume for the author himself, the greedy fellow may even raise the price. All the people here in this city, they are all, all of them, rogues and hypocrites."

"Oh, they're not a bad lot, once you get to know them. I rather enjoyed myself when I was here, could tell you some adventures that would rival those of my father! Wait until you have had better fortune, Master Mozart, and you will come to love this city as I do."

We had arrived at the chemist's. It did not give the impression of being open, despite Raaff's report.

I knocked vigorously on the shutters. To come this far and not—

From inside, a hacking cough rose, a voice quavering that he was coming, was coming. Soon thereafter, a scraggly head emerged from behind a door.

I begged his pardon for the disturbance, but a patient was in urgent need of some *pulvis epilepticus niger.* Perhaps he had some for sale?

"Never heard of it. *Niger?* Got charcoal in it? I can offer a mix that has some charcoal in it, if it's digestive troubles you're trying to mend."

"Not only digestive," I said.

"Well, I have none of that *epilepticus* stuff. What's in it? Maybe we call it here by another name."

I detailed its contents, the black powder my father always carried with him on our journeys in his medicine chest, the remedy he had been unable to resupply us with despite my entreaties of the past two months. Desiccated earthworms were the primary ingredient, along with charcoal, of course. But also deer's antler, myrrh, coral, frogs' heads, and placenta.

"A goodly brew, but I have none, alas. Anything else that may tickle your fancy?"

"Margrave powder?"

"An excellent purgative, but we are missing iris roots and pinches of magnesium of late and thus cannot provide the right mix. And the right mix, in any profession, is the road to success, the right balance. Two weeks from now I am expecting a shipment of the missing ingredients and will be able to provide satisfaction."

I had been in every apothecary's and to every chemist in Paris—or so it seemed—walking through the mud for hours, but nobody peddled the black powder, only black souls everywhere, everywhere.

I set out for home, Jack Taylor at my heels.

"You are not well, Master Mozart?"

I hesitated, shrugged my shoulders, continued quickly up the street. So quickly that I stubbed my toe on a stupid slab of cobblestone. I would have fallen—and scraped and torn and tattered my britches—if Jack Taylor's swift hand had not darted out and steadied me. The dusty light of a growing moon revealed a smile, the sort that a brother might attempt at his younger sibling's awkwardness, the sort of brother that Providence had never given me.

"You must tell me what ails you, young Mozart."

"My mother has not been well. When we arrived at the end of winter, she was ill, suffered from toothache, sore throat, her ears throbbed—a recurrence of a previous catarrh. The last of our black powder worked wonders, and she seemed to recover. Then, recently, her disorder came back, worse than before, and this time we had run out of our favorite remedy and—"

"Was she bled?"

"Copiously, last week. Two platefuls. But two days ago...No matter."

No matter indeed. Diarrhea, nonstop diarrhea, not something I cared to describe or discuss with Taylor.

"And what do the doctors say?"

What could I answer? That no doctor had said a word, not one opinion had been pronounced, not one drop of medicine purchased? Because I could not pay for a physick or a sip of syrup or heaven knew what else? Answer that? That I am too poor to afford a medical opinion? And that even if I could afford one, Maman would not accept a French doctor, that she demanded someone from Germany—and that it was this unreasonable demand that had allowed me, thus far, to hide from her the fact that I was unable to engage

the services of a physician of any sort or language, even if
he came from darkest Africa. Just as I could not tell her
that I was too proud to ask Baron von Grimm or Madame
d'Épinay for help, already too indebted in too many ways,
could not tell her that I would not see either of them until
I had paid back my loan, until Baron von Grimm ceased
sending Papa insulting letters about my lack of cunning and
shrewdness and entrepreneurial spirit, that I seemed to be
on an eternal holiday, repeating to me my father's injunc-
tions to ingratiate myself with people of standing, to follow
the latest fashion, to please, please, please the rich.

"The doctors are not sure," I said. "Opinions vary."

He understood. He had seen his fill of patients with not
a farthing to their name. I was no different from the beggar
boy with fistula lacrymalis, only easier to humiliate. Jack
Taylor knew sorrow when it overflows, he had witnessed his
share of desperate men and sightless women, he had given
hope and taken hope away, he was as much an expert in
cheer and grief and pain as any musician, he had comforted
helpless relatives, he knew no matter how much he prescribed and operated and consoled, he would lose, all of us
would, the battle against the condition called by a word he
did not like to use, that I did not dare pronounce but that
lay between us, as it had a mere short while ago when the
beggar boy had thrust his bony fingers at us.

Jack Taylor did not offer immediately to attend Maman,
and we both knew why. The London Bach had accused Jack's
father, the Chevalier, of murder or, if that was a feverish

exaggeration, of horrendous bungling, but the accusation made Jack Taylor wary of intervening, he wanted to make sure that, in case anything drastic happened to my mother, he would be held blameless. If a death were to occur—there, the word had been formulated, even if only inside my despairing brain—it, at least, could not be laid at his door.

"I have a friend, a French physician, a certain Landru, devoted to me since my years in Paris. He owes me many a favor from when we were lads and I extricated him from boudoir predicaments that I will not tire you with. He was then a lover of music and must be so now and undoubtedly is aware, as all of Paris is, of your exploits. I am sure he would be glad to visit your esteemed mother, doing it merely for love of you, repaid only by your eventual promise to come to his home one day and regale him with one of your sonatas. Would you allow me to contact him?"

"My mother will not tolerate a doctor from France, only one who speaks German." I sighed, relieved at being able to tell him something that was true. "I am at a loss at how to proceed."

We had turned off la rue Réamur and there we were, at last, in front of 6 rue de Gros Chenet.

"If your mother is further afflicted, please do not hesitate to call on me. I am staying at the Hotel de Bretagne, rue Croix-des-Petits-Champs."

I did not comment that this was the very lodging announced by Johann Christian for his Paris sojourn. Perhaps Taylor knew, perhaps he didn't. With any luck, they'd meet in the corridor one day and it would no longer fall upon me to bring them together or keep them apart. An enormous fatigue descended on me, heavy like a Buxtehude organ recital. I can't recall if I even said good-bye to him. Taylor had accompanied me to my quarters, he could find me again, he would not be leaving Paris soon. At that point, all I wanted was to climb the stairs and see Maman.

She was waiting up for me. No matter how late I arrived. She did not go out during the day, afraid of the dirty streets, stubbornly unwilling to learn even one word of French, only once in the past month venturing forth for an outing to the Luxembourg Gardens with Gertrude Heina—Maman could not say no, she was in debt, as I am, to Madame Heina for publishing my symphonies—and my dear mother had come back much restored, recounting to me later each statue of female heroines and saints erected by Maria de Medicis, each flower, each ugly look by a gardener when she had pressed forward to smell the scent. *Why not go out more, Maman?* But she would not yield, she enjoyed the safety of her room, no matter how dark it might be, how dreary the little courtyard. She was grateful, naturally, for her occasional visitors, remembering the details of their conversations minutely—a prelude to my telling her of my day, with whom had I lunched, how had the lessons gone, how was Noverre's ballet *Les Petits Riens* coming along, had I met the eminent Benjamin Franklin yet, what news of the possible war between England and France, would Prussia, would Austria be involved, why should we care about the American colonies, she said severely, why should the declaration of their independence in that faraway barbarous land affect us, what affair was it of ours, was it true, she would ask, that people back home were being whipped off the streets and pulled out of their beds to be turned into soldiers, was the price of truffles still exorbitant, had I found any black powder at the chemist's? And then, what mattered most, the one query she really cared about: What had I composed—a pity that we could not have a clavier brought up through the narrow stairs and hall, though the air was good in this neighborhood, she had to admit that—what marvels had I worked on at the Legros residence, she trusted that my host had not interrupted me too often with his virtuoso, albeit strident, bel canto, oh, what a pity that we had not more privacy of our own, but you will have created something for me, no?

I had, I had. I would play the melodies on the violin, often sing the tunes. Singing, invariably at the end of my narration of the day, was her favorite, as it led to our dance of the night: we would whirl and twirl around the constricted floor, expertly sidestepping the chairs and the bed and the walls, once in a while bumping a commode with her butt and then mine, laughing and farting. It was the part of the ceremony she enjoyed most, most looked forward to.

That night I found her wan and weary, exhausted from the incessant waters she was exuding. To cheer her up, I sang an aria I had made for Aloysia Weber when I had given her lessons some months ago in Mannheim—Maman did not like Aloysia, much preferring her sister, Constanze—but she loved the aria and would chip in with a delicate ritornello and echo. But not tonight. Tonight she was too tired. No jokes about shit, no butts against commodes, no silliness.

We did a slight minuet, tiptoeing from one end of the room to the other, and then, dizzy, breathing heavily, she motioned to her bed, asked me to help her undress and fit on her nightgown, and then slipped between the covers.

She would never get up again.

Our last dance in Paris, that night.

The next day, June 19, was impossibly, improbably, eternally long. First stop, the pawnbroker on rue des Jeuners— the golden snuffbox and the watch chain I had won that glorious, baffling night at Dean Street, gone down the hatch and into the vaults of the shop, though I at least had the satisfaction of negotiating the price up a bit, browbeating the man into adding a louis d'or to my ticket. I knew I would not see them again except displayed in that window one month from now when I failed to redeem them, would look into that window as if I were watching my own fading and unredeemable memories. No matter. The money jangling in my pocket allowed me a visit to the butcher's for a shoulder of lamb and then to the baker's so he could roast it and have it delivered to rue du Gros Chenet, and finally a detour through the confectionary for a selection of delicacies for Maman.

She was still not awake when I returned with some bread and some good butter, the one that costs forty sous, not the dreadful kind that is merely disguised and indigestible lard.

I leaned over her and noted that her breathing was not that irregular, left her some coins on the nightstand so she could send the servant next door to purchase some wine perhaps, perhaps a young chicken, a couple of turnips, even truffles, whatever she might fancy.

And then, the rest of the day. An endless, tedious lesson with the daughter of the Duc de Guines—all in vain, as she will never be a composer, for she is not only thoroughly stupid but also thoroughly lazy. So, off to put the finishing touches to my sonata, the one in A minor, on the Legros piano—even if I have no commission for it, even if no one will pay me a penny for the whole thing. It must be ready for Johann Christian. I believe he will appreciate it, he will understand where I am heading with it, he will absorb the...

Then, a late lunch at Count Van Sickengen's—the hours passed quickly, it was such a pleasure to spend some time with a true connoisseur and passionate lover of music. He had some operatic scores that we went through at length, analyzing, praising, admiring, until he finally brought out *Demofoonte*, Metastasio's libretto—not much to my liking, as it is interspersed with choruses and dances, a typical adaption for the French stage. If only I could find the right text for my opera, the Count believed a commission might be in the offing. By the time we were done, it was close to eight in the evening, and I hastened home.

Jack Taylor was there, in front of the house. Recalling his vigil at King's Court Square, outside the London Bach's Dean Street residence, I wondered if he had been waiting since morning, if he would have waited for days in order to see me. But it was not to further his interests that he was loitering this time, but in order to further mine.

"This is for you," he said, without even the preamble of a greeting, so anxious was he to hand me the first package of two he was carrying.

I opened it.

Inside was the copy of my father's *Violinschule* instruction book that I had inquired about a mere twenty-four hours ago.

"As the music shop owner did not associate me with you, I managed to parley a less lavish price, Master Mozart," he said, and seemed almost contrite. "So no need to repay me, it goes without saying. Take it as a token of my esteem, a way of apologizing for the forced absence of the doctor I assured you could visit your honorable mother. Alas, that boyhood friend I spoke of, Dr. Alphonse Landru, is in the Bastille. For a pamphlet he wrote against despotism. He was always rather rebellious and now only has fellow prisoners to heal. But I did not relent in my quest. I sought out a brother of his, also a physician—and he, Paul Landru—our bad luck does not abate—had passed away. The smallpox. So it goes. We ourselves, who stave off illness, are not immune when our time is come. My father himself, in this same city—he died blind, as if the Good Lord were somehow mocking him. He had restored the beauties of the orb to so many, yet ended his days sightless. It is as if you were struck deaf, Master Mozart, imagine a deaf musician, what greater calamity can there be? But let us think of gladder things. Such as this gift from London."

He handed me the second package.

And there were the buttons, the mother-of-pearl buttons I had not been able to convince my Papa to acquire, the buttons I intended to show off in the Tuileries as soon as I was able to get a seamstress to sew them on, though maybe that would not be necessary. Maman loved to sew and—but, oh dear, she had ceased doing so over the past few months due to the ache in her eyes and the weakness of her fingers. This ought to cheer her up. No more knitting, I'd say—you've been knitting away interminably, how about these buttons, huh? Oh yes, I had not been wrong: Jack Taylor would bring us luck, would bring us health.

I thanked him profusely and, not willing to let another second go by, hastily bidding him adieu, bounded up the stairs.

Maman was worse than before.

She had not touched the roast, the bread was buttered but only a bite had been nibbled from it, a tiny morsel of a crust, the money for sweets was where I had left it earlier in the day with such high hopes.

But at least she had not gone to sleep, was waiting for my report of activities, and her eyes shone slightly when I spoke about the praise from Van Sickengen, lit up truly and sincerely when I sang one of the themes from the A-minor sonata. I sat by her on the bed and took her fingers and danced them with mine across the pillow next to the sweaty web of her hair and then stopped when she said her hands hurt too much to continue.

And the coughing, the fever, the diarrhea, her headache, her lovely head was aching and exploding—worse, ever worse, the following morn. "I must call a doctor," I said firmly, even if it meant appealing to shrill Baron von Grimm, endure his perpetual lecturing.

"Only if he is German. I will not see one of the foppish French quacks, all flourishes and empty bowing. They know nothing about our Austrian bodies and requirements. I must be able to interrogate him in my own language, understand what he is saying, so no one can hide the truth of my condition. German, or nothing."

I had to go out that Saturday to again see Madame la Duchesse de Chabot, hoping she would finally recommend me to the Duchesse de Bourbon, who has connections to the court. If she could get her father, Orleans, to put in a good word with his cousin, the King…I had been there before, in late winter, when the Chabot woman made me wait for hours in an ice-cold, unheated room that hadn't even a fireplace. And all the windows and doors to the frosty garden, open! She ultimately appeared and pointed to an old, dilapidated clavier and requested that I play something, anything, a bagatelle, a *petit rien*. I suggested that we go to someplace warm, as my fingers were numb. She agreed, "*Oh oui, Monsieur, vous avez raison,*" but instead of guiding me elsewhere, sat down to draw, which she continued to do for a whole hour, amused by the company of some gentlemen who arrived laughing and perhaps inebriated and then lounged around, praising her skin and the shape of her bodice. I decided to finally play on the wretched pianoforte, in case that would gain her attention. Not a whit. She kept on drawing and the men kept on laughing, so I was really playing to the chairs, the tables, the walls. Did it make a difference that I received, when I was finally done, a shower of éloges? *Oh, mais c'est un prodige, c'est inconcevable, c'est étonnant!* And that was it—adieu. Come back in the summer, good Maestro, when your fingers are not so frozen over. Come back? Never, never!

Never is a word someone in my position should not utter, let alone think.

Because that Saturday morning a perfumed message had been remitted to la rue de Gros Chenet. Congratulations from the Duchesse de Chabot on my recent success at the Concert Spirituel. Apparently there was a notice about it in the *Courier de l'Europe*. So now she wanted to cultivate my friendship! I was too desperately in need of support to ignore her summons. But it was all a sham. I did not even meet the lady, let alone get the accursed recommendation. Two dour footmen relegated me to the same gloomy gallery as before, except that this time the doors and windows were closed, with no breeze, consequently, to relieve the heat. I waited for an hour, roused one of the servants, and asked him if he was waiting for winter to open the room up. He did not even crack a smile at this joke. "Besides a piper, sir," the ogre said, "are you also now an architect who presumes to give advice on how a palace like this should be built?"

I ignored his insolence, demanded to know when the Duchesse would receive me.

He said she had unfortunately been called away on an urgent errand and would be back that evening. Before leaving, she had graciously indicated that I might wait for her in the kitchen and be served some soup.

My answer to him—and to his mistress—was to sit myself down at the selfsame derelict clavier and, playing like a fiend, belt out the words "Whoever does not want me can lick my ass!" I did this in Italian first, then in French, and finally in German, and then departed before they could throw me out.

The German words echoed in my head as I trudged back home through the rain and mud—yes, it had started raining—those words my mother had taught me, that she would never joke about again unless...unless...a German doctor. Unless I found a German doctor. Or a doctor who spoke German!

That was it. That was the solution!

As I was thoroughly soaked and had to traverse the Faubourg St. Germain on my way home, what did it matter if I added a few minutes to my itinerary and stopped at the Hotel de Bretagne?

Dr. Taylor was not in, I was informed by the majordomo.

I left him a message, asking him to call on me at Gros Chenet, but to please make sure we spoke outside the hearing range of my mother—as if she could hear very much, poor thing.

He diligently obeyed my request when he appeared two days later—it was a Monday, early in the morning. We spoke downstairs, in the courtyard. I kept looking up at the window, in case Maman had risen from bed and was spying on me, trying to figure out who this stranger was.

I explained my plan to Jack Taylor. He was not a German doctor, but he did speak German, and, according to everything he had told me, he was a doctor, the third generation in his family to practice the profession. True, his specialty were the eyes, but had he not mentioned once that the eyes were the windows of the soul and the jewels of the body, could he not at least give me an opinion as to what affected my mother?

He consented without a second thought. So rapidly that I wondered if he was not calculating his every move, placing me henceforth in his debt, so that I might not refuse, when the moment came, to act as a bridge to the elusive Christel when my mentor finally arrived in Paris.

Did it matter?

Maman was so pleased to make his acquaintance, complimented the good doctor on his German and chattered away with him for an hour as if they were old friends.

He examined her thoroughly, prescribed antispasmodic powders that he happened to have in his bag, held her hand and lied to her, saying she would get better, of course she would, and then stood up, and for the first time since he had entered the room, met my own eyes, and repeated the same lie to me, of course, your Maman will get better, Master

Mozart, knowing, both of us, that it was not true, knowing, both of us, that she was dying and that there was nothing he or I or any other earthly power could do to save her.

It was the last long conversation she was to have with anyone in this sad world of ours.

The next day—was it Tuesday by then, Wednesday? I began to lose count—she was stricken with deafness, was so hoarse I could not understand a word she was coughing up.

He came again, Jack Taylor did, aware that I was more grateful for his company than for his opinion, which coincided with that of the doctor that Baron von Grimm finally sent over. Internal inflammation, they both murmured, Jack and this other fellow. Internal inflammation, what did it mean? I had been inside her for many months, I had sought refuge in her arms for many years, how could I not find a way now to rid her of the demon fever that was eating her every cell, shattering her heart, plunging her into a delirium that lasted for hours, days, a whole week?

He was there, Jack Taylor, when I brought a German priest to see her. He waited with me outside the door while the man heard her last confession—what could he hear if she could not speak, what could she confess if she had never hurt anyone on this earth, why was he giving her extreme unction instead of hope?

When she lapsed into a coma from which she did not awake, only then did Jake Taylor finally leave.

He had spent the past two days and nights by my side and by hers and now, incredibly, wisely, tactfully, decided that such intimate moments should not be marred with the slightest hint of a stranger's imposition.

Five hours later, Maman was dead.

I had asked her, as a child, Will you be here for me, Maman? Will you always be here for me?

And she had answered, over and over, I will never leave your side, Woferl, I will always be near and here and dear for you.

Do you promise, Maman?

I promise.

A real promise?

A real promise, Wolfgang Amadeus Mozart—lover of God, destined to make this world a wondrous place.

She had broken her promise and my heart, my heart, my heart was broken—and only she could mend it, she who left me alone forever and ever amen on July 3, 1778, at 10:21 at night.

I cannot remember what happened during the everlasting night that followed.

Apparently, I wrote to my father telling him that his dear Maria Anna was ill but that we still had the expectation that she would recover. Apparently, I then wrote a second letter to the Abbé Bullinger in Salzburg, informing him of the terrible news and begging him to prepare Papa and Nannerl. Apparently, I sent both letters by the same mail coach. Apparently, apparently, because I have no memory of what I did or what I wrote, apparently, apparently, because all was appearance and illusion and shadow during those days.

I have a vague recollection of her burial in the Church
of St. Eustache. Not who was there, though it must have
been Francois Heina, so loyal in those last days, and maybe
his wife, Gertrude, perhaps our friend Anton Raaff, whose
beatific voice must have been muffled as he held me in his
arms and whispered consolation. Not Jack Taylor, I think—
or was he lurking nearby, as was his wont, unwilling to disturb this new young brother he had made in Paris, perhaps
recalling his own father's death six years earlier, recalling his
mother's in London when the Chevalier was abroad?

I really don't know. The only image I can gather from
that funeral occasion is of the statue of the Holy Mother,
the Virgin who had not listened to my prayers, who—but
I swept the thought from my mind and my black heart. I
could not, not now, not ever, especially not now, doubt the
goodness of God, doubt that I would meet Maman again
soon, that she was waiting for me in a better world. Otherwise I would, I would, I would—what?

How sick and crazed was I?

So sick, so crazed that, for the first time in my life, music
was denied to me.

And in its place came a series of reproaches that I had
no defense against, that poured into the emptiness left behind by the ultimate silence that denied the possibility of
beauty, that denied the promise of healing music with which
I had populated the earth and air.

Had I done enough to save her? If she had stayed behind
in Salzburg, would she still be alive? If I had stayed behind,

if I, Woferl, Wolfgangerl, Wolfgang, me, me, me, would she still be alive?

These were not questions I wanted to ask myself, but they were questions my father would hound me with in his first letter of reproof when he finally heard of his wife's demise, and then in a second letter and a third one, and then would continue asking me when we met in Salzburg, if ever, that is, I went back, as I must, as I had to in order to comfort him and my sister—but what was I to say, what? You were the one, Papa, who demanded that she accompany me to Mannheim first and then to Paris, you were the one who did not allow her to come home when she was not feeling well, you were the one who would not trust me to be by myself, you were the one who was afraid of the women I might meet and be seduced by, other families I might befriend? No, no, all that would remain unsaid, I was loath to harass him as he would harass me. Even so, I had to return, I had debts of many sorts to pay, not just money debts. It was unthinkable to remain in dreadful Paris, and yet I did not wish to regress to suffocating, provincial Salzburg and the Prince Archbishop's capricious demands, his thin lips and even thinner purse. And why stay here or why go back or continue on to anywhere at all if I—if I could no longer compose, if the ceaseless, seemingly endless waterfall of music had, in fact, ceased and desisted and ended?

I had never had to ask myself what so many ask themselves at an early age and then as they grow up and later as they decline: Why am I here? Why was I, of all possible gardens of people, put on this earth, for what purpose?

The answer for me had been clear before I could even formulate the idea, was so obvious it did not require articulation.

I was here to fill the world with myself and the joy of the sweetest, deepest sounds I could imagine.

I was here to prove God's goodness simply by sitting at a clavier and letting the air welcome the sounds, let the universe breathe me into existence as my imagination overflowed like a fountain, like a flood, like a lake and a sea and an ocean.

Such music had not been created turning my back on death.

I had seen the jaws of extinction close by—perhaps on the very day I was born, perhaps as soon as I left Maman and cried out into the wilderness of the world, I had seen death approaching along with my first breath. And that cry of mine may not have been divinely inspired, may not have been conceived in beauty, but it was a first attempt to defy the void, a way for me to postpone its reign and humble its pride. And ever since, each time death's handmaidens, sickness and fever and diarrhea and delirium, had crept into my life and threatened me and my beloved family, I had responded with music and more music.

So automatic and effortless had this mother source of love been that I had taken it for granted, did not guess that it could ever stagnate, could not know that behind and below the music, deep within the quiet, dark core inside me, that plague of questions, why, why, why, was waiting, the questions that, with Maman's death, I was no longer shielded from.

Without music, I had become an ordinary man.

Just someone who, like every one of us on this orb, must lose a mother and someday a father, like everyone else become an orphan, all of us orphans wandering the land and the waves, and someday die, like everyone else, unprotected, naked as the day we had arrived, with no one to promise she would be there always, would always be there for me.

Sick, crazed, yes, abandoned by the guardian angel of my music.

Anton Raaff, good soul that he was, tried to revive my spirits, sang my own songs back to me, sat me down at a clavier in his lodgings, pushed me to compose.

But when he was gone to Rome on July 10—one full week after Maman had left me, one full week after Maman had broken her promise—it was then that Jack Taylor gently edged his way back into my life.

His recurring presence was a particular boon to me. As someone who had been through such losses himself, he knew when to leave me to mourn by myself, the better to re-create in solitude the face and gestures and voice of the departed—and also knew when I would need company so the solitude would not swallow me. Even more so when my mood darkened again at the news I received, in early August, of another death. Someone my age. Someone exactly my age. Twenty-two brief years. Someone who was as dear to me—because unique, because there was no one that talented, the

only other prodigy as a child I ever met—as my own soul
and mirror. So close to me that they called him the London Mozart. Thomas Linley, my dear Tomassino, had been
drowned in a lake near Castle Grimsthorpe in England. We
had wept bitter tears when we had parted in Florence eight
years earlier. Just one Italian week we spent together on this
earth, playing duets and playing games and singing arias
with our fabulous Manzuoli, who gave free lessons to me as
he had in London and to Tomassino out of love for me, we
swore, Linley and I, that we would soon be reunited. And
reunited we might be, if death came for me as it had for him,
the sooner the better.

And to whom confide what I was going through? There
was no one other than Jack Taylor, no one else surrounding
me who was not in contact with my father, everyone else
acting as my father's messenger. Only Jack Taylor was mine,
entirely on my side, more indispensable to me from the
moment I absconded from the Gros Chenet lodgings that
had such terrible memories and moved back—what other
alternative did a penniless mute composer have?—with
Baron von Grimm and his censorious eyes and tongue. Jack
Taylor—close enough to be of solace, enough of a stranger
so as not to get entangled in the web of intrigue spun by family and friends—nursed me back to health.

He began by taking my mind off the immediate, despondent, dogged thoughts that would not leave me alone.

By regaling me with stories of the Chevalier and his
adventures.

He soon was able to apprehend that one thing and one thing only interested me, quickened me, in those tales. Not his father's triumphs in the court of Parma or a spectacular eye surgery performed in Vienna. I had been there, done that, seen that Empress, had the Marquise of So-and-So bow to me. He saw that my eyes sparkled, for the first time in many days, when he recounted how a ninety-year-old woman had offered to marry the debonair Chevalier, how a sixteen-year-old virgin had rendered her body to his graces when her vision had been restored so her limbs could thank what her eyes could now see, how Jack's father had introduced a young gentleman into a nunnery and the consequences thereof, how a lady of quality had come by the Chevalier's lodgings, disguised, unwilling to disclose her identity until the fullness of her torso and breasts revealed all, how he danced with a princess and almost had his head cut off for his effrontery, and so on and on, ever more bawdy stories—three men and one woman in a bed, three women and one man, dwarfs and bearded ladies and hermaphrodites, extravaganzas that obviously no longer derived from his memories of the Chevalier's exploits but that he had lifted from who knows what books. Some of his more graphic and exhaustive scenes I recognized from the yarns of Restif de la Bretonne, *Le Pied de Fanchette* and *Le Paysan Perverti*, which I had already read on my own. But I did not care that he was now inventing all this coupling, borrowing from every fictional or real source at his disposal in order to invigorate me again, get my blood red-hot, my juices flowing, my spirits and other things up, up, up, he said.

He must have sensed that I was mending, because one day, as we strolled down la rue d'Assas, he dared to ask me, without preamble: "Are you in love, young Master Mozart?"

I did not hesitate.

"Yes."

"Tell me about her."

"Not one. Two, I'm in love with two girls." And added: "Each different from the other," in case he had misunderstood my meaning.

"Tell me."

"One is virtuous and chaste and sings like an angel. Her name is Aloysia and I would like to bring her here to Paris or to London if ever I return to settle there, bring her and her delightful family, the Webers. Sheer folly, Mr. Taylor, as you have realized that I cannot support even my own miserable self, cannot even afford a room of my own. But there you have it."

"And the other?"

"I have explored every hole in her body, every infinite cavity, why not, why not, why not," I said. "She has no musical talents but smiles me into existence every time I see her face and with every funny letter we exchange, responding to my nonsense with no sense of her own, why not her?"

"And her name?"

"Anna Maria, but I call her Basle, little cousin, because she is the daughter of my father's brother."

"And you would also bring her to Paris and London and...?"

"I do not know. How can I know? How can I even know if I love Aloysia anymore? How can I know anything?"

He saw I was slipping once again into a pit of helplessness, again beginning to feel sorry for myself, and he swiftly countered:

"Then wait, dear friend. Wait for the woman who is your singing angel and your bodily inspiration, wait for the one face that will combine all that you wish. She is there, she will come to you, she will console you for every loss and make you understand the true meaning of tenderness, shall invite you into the threshold of paradise."

"Do you really believe that is possible?"

"It is what you need and what you deserve."

"These two do not often go together in this unjust world of ours."

"She is there, I tell you. She will be an angel, I tell you, but just make sure she is an angel that knows how to please and pleasure you, splendorously, gloriously, endlessly, just make sure she's an angel who, in a word, knows how to fuck."

I smiled at this—my first smile in weeks.

And then, guessing that I was ready for what he would next volunteer, he took me by the shoulders and sat me down. We were in the Luxembourg Gardens, where Maman had last inhaled the fresh air of freedom, under the statues of all those female goddesses, that is where he chose to shake me out of the lethargy that had seduced me with its swan calls.

"You can never let despair seize you by the throat," he said, echoing Carl Friedrich Abel from a dinner so long ago it seemed to have been lived by someone else. And then: "You can live without your mother, dear Wolfgang. All of us can manage it somehow, though we swore it would not, could not, be. But you cannot live, my friend, without your music. Find your music again and you will find your mother. Even if she cannot presently hear you. Though how do you know that she cannot? How do you know that she is not close by and dies more every day because your notes do not accompany her on the final stages of her soul's journey? How can you make her so unhappy and lonely in death"—it was the first time he had ever pronounced that forbidden word—"when she was the one who gave you life, carried you inside her, as you must now carry her? Turn your love for her into beauty, Wolfgang, your sorrow, your questions, your grief, your hopes, even your lust. Find her in your music now, and then tomorrow and the day after as a way of paving the road to your final reunion, the final reunion we all so desire. But if you do not start this quest soon, that road will itself disappear from lack of use. Paths must be trod often to stay alive. They are like legs and members and eyes. What could hurt your Maman more than seeing that her absence has destroyed you?"

And so I started to recover.

But even as I coaxed out the first melodies, went back to work on my A-minor piano sonata, even as I gradually became the young Mozart I had always been—even allowed myself a prank or two, a joke or three—even then, there still remained inside and outside a question that had no answer, not even in my music as it stirred itself like a brew into life.

I had asked the Virgin for help and had received none. I had prayed to God through her to grant me one favor, just one, if my art pleased Him, pleased His mother.

His response had been a slap in the face, a cough in the night, a load of blood and shit spilling out of my mother, soiling my mother and soiling the world.

Who was this God acting in this cruel, inscrutable way? How to continue believing in His Benevolence? What was His true face? How to tell Him from the Devil? How to get Him to reveal Himself and, with that revelation, confirm that there was truly a meaning to my life on this earth?

When I managed, one evening, on a day in mid-August to bring these doubts to the surface and lay them before Jack Taylor as we drank far into the night at a tavern on la rue St. André des Arts that he had frequented as a student and that was still doing brisk business thirty years later, when he heard me out until I was as drained and silent as the god who had endowed me with a mother only to take her away, awarded me so much talent only to force me to realize how easy it would be to take everything away, that is when Jack Taylor surprised me by flashing a smile at my misery. And surprised me even more by returning unabashedly to his obsession, what he had not mentioned once since our first encounter after the concert on Corpus Christi, the reason for this visit to Paris, the reason for introducing himself during the winter storm of London, the reason he happened to be here to console me.

Jack Taylor said, with utter simplicity and perfect candor:

"That is the question, precisely, those are the questions, dear Wolfgang, that my father and Johann Sebastian Bach discussed before the Chevalier performed a second operation on his eyes—because he operated not once but twice on your mentor's father, perhaps you did not know that?"

I did but preferred not to dampen his prospects of seeing Christel by repeating the traumatic account of that second operation. So I asked something that had been flitting about in my head for all these years: "And Handel? How is this related to Handel?"

"He is also included in this story," said Jack Taylor, "as Johann Christian knows all too well—and as he will have to admit when he arrives in Paris soon, soon, oh so soon."

Had he tended to me so fondly so I would do his bidding and arrange that long-sought-after meeting? I would not have chided him for pursuing his own best interests, as all men and most women are inclined. And yet, I cannot relinquish the certainty that he was genuinely concerned about me, as a man and as a healer, that he really liked me and felt it his duty—nay, his deepest aspiration—to offer relief when I was most lost and confused. Bless him, at any rate, for the hours he spent by my side. Bless him for being there when Maman could no longer keep her promise.

And thus it was that my fate became entwined with his, became entwined with the fate of the London Bach, thus it was that I prepared myself to finally bring together the two sons, the son of the Chevalier John Taylor, servant of Kings, and the son of Johann Sebastian Bach, servant of God.

Twenty-eight years after their fathers had so violently and enigmatically met, I brought them face-to-face, I arranged that encounter where I found out what had really happened to the eyes of the elder Bach before he died in Leipzig.

Minuetto and Finale

As a token of my esteem for Johann Christian Bach after so many years of separation, I had two gifts for his discerning ears—two gifts, quite apart from the evident pleasure he received from my own warm welcome.

Without losing the original reason for both musical offerings—I wanted to please him, I wanted his opinion, I wanted him to remark how much I had learned from him and how much I had distanced myself from his work—there was now added something else: they were part of my strategy to get him to accept an interview with Jack Taylor.

There we were, chatting as if the concert at Carlisle House had been yesterday, there we were in the salon the Hotel de Bretagne had set aside for Herr Bach to work in, quiet and cool, away from the drenching heat of August.

"If you will allow, Maestro," I said, and sat myself down at the clavier that had been impatiently awaiting the flutter of my fingers. But instead of playing on the keyboard, I had, animated by my usual flair for the dramatic gesture, clapped my hands, and none other than Sophie Arnould, the greatest French soprano of all time, entered the room. Just four years before my visit to Paris, she had conquered *le tout Paris* in Gluck's *Orfeo et Eurydice*, but her voice and health had declined since then, and she was, therefore, delighted—hoping for a role in Johann Christian's upcoming opera—when I requested her presence to sing for Baron Bach.

And sing she did. The words were the ones I had heard wafting through the chill air of my London childhood on that night I had found myself for the first time alone—an anticipation of a more tragic and solitary night that would waylay me in the future of Paris thirteen years later—those verses had been sung by Clementina and accompanied by the viola da gamba that Christian was teasing melodies from for that occasion. They had stayed with me, those stanzas by Metastasio, "*Non so d' onde viene*," that iciness in the heart, those conflicting emotions I could not express back then, but when I had fallen in love with Aloysia Weber during my earlier *séjour* in Mannheim, I had then set them to my own music. Meant both as an homage to my mentor, the London Bach, and as a declaration of independence from him. The aria was my way of asking for his pity, *la sola pietà*, asking him, through the singer, to forgive my troubled soul, hoping he would not mind that I had stolen the very words he had once used for his own song, employing them now to show him and the world that I had surpassed my own teacher.

When she was done and had left the room, effervescent with the praise we had sprinkled on her, Christian allowed a smile of gratitude to lighten his face.

And had but two generous words as a response to my aria, my challenge, my dare.

"Thank you," he said.

That was all.

And that was enough.

What more does a father want for his child than for the child to be better, to go further, to honor the father's eternal influence by going beyond what the father had ever dreamt?

But there was, in effect, more.

I was still at the piano. Took a deep breath and then...

The first chords of the Allegro Maestoso from the A-minor sonata! Would he understand this, the pain? Would he understand this, my brooding heart? Would he understand this, the dissonance? Would he? Would he? And if he did, what would he make then of the Andante Cantabile con Espressione, the good-bye that has not yet said hello, the hello that wants never to say good-bye? Would he, would he? Would the storm submerge him, demand too much, break bonds between us by forcing him to face demons that I was letting loose and that he, like all mortal men, sensed raging unappeasably inside? Would he understand, would he, would he? That solace and shadows go together, that sorrow is our fate if we are to love, the price we pay for loving too much and too well and too deeply in the pit we have dug for ourselves? And then the Presto—oh yes, I was answering that symphony of his he had created to introduce my own symphony more than a decade ago in Carlisle House, I was repeating the three movements of that faraway symphony of mine, the first I had ever composed, the same names for the same movements, but how different now was this Mozart at the piano in Paris, how far had I come, too far, too far, perhaps too far, if he did not understand then who would, who would understand that this was what I was brought into the world to do, what we were all brought into the world to do, and that I had been blessed and cursed with this task and that I would see it through, hurry it through, slow it through, to the bitter, joyful end? Would he, would he? Would he understand that this was the rhythm of the Universe that my mother had taught me with each beat of her heart that would someday die as I swam my way to this moment, this music, this Allegro and Andante and Presto, that we can keep the terrors at bay but only for the interlude and span of this brief sonata of life, that we will die and that there is nothing we can do about it, would he, would he?

And then the piano quieted down and my hands rested, who knows if forever, on my friend the keyboard, and I was finished, if anything can ever be truly finished in life except life itself.

I did not dare to look at my mentor.

A long silence and then his voice.

"My condolences," he said.

Nothing more.

Nothing more, save that he was crying.

And I cried along with him.

He came up to me, took me into his arms. "Has it been hard?" he whispered in my ear.

This was the opening I had been hoping for—a chance to respond yes, very hard, but thanks to an unexpected friend from the past I had managed to—but so calculated a gambit was too cunningly removed from what I was feeling and Bach was feeling, both of us still soaked in the turbulence and quietude of my work. Another occasion would present itself when I could bring up Jack Taylor and how he had helped me to survive the month and a half that followed my mother's death.

I disengaged from my mentor, stood up, walked to the large window of the room.

"That word," I said. "I have been thinking about it."

"Condolences."

"Yes. It comes from the Latin, as I am sure you know, Maestro. *Con* and *dolere*, to feel pain with, to be in sympathy with someone else's pain. And I have been wondering if all music, the best music, the kind you and I create, if what we do and what your father and what Handel and Scarlatti, Vivaldi and Rameau did, and Haydn still does, bless him, all that harmony, is not one long condolence to our fellow men, one desperate attempt to accompany and alleviate their pain, the fact that they and we must die, express that pain and vanquish it through a shared territory of perfection, an

inkling of immortality to counter our sad fate. That is what
I have been wondering."

Christian laughed heartily, and I loved that laugh, I had
forgotten how much I loved it and missed it.

"There is no need for such elaborate philosophizing. Da
capo, da capo, bravissimo. What you played right now—I
have never heard anything like it. Unique, it is unique."

My emotions now under control, I saw another possible
chance to refer, however indirectly, to the Chevalier. "Not
even from your father?" I asked.

"Perhaps, but in him it was not so—personal, I suppose
is the word I am looking for. Listening to his music, you
have the sense that he would have composed it in exactly
the same manner if he had been blessed with seven children instead of twenty, if only one had survived of those
twenty rather than ten, or if he had not generated even one
son or daughter, like Handel. I am certain that my father
would have written his *Passions* and his *Easter Oratorio* and
his *Coffee Cantata*, if there had been no King of Prussia and
no sovereign at Weimar, that very selfsame stream of pro-
ductions if he had been on top of a mountain instead of in
Leipzig. Except, perhaps, at the end. At the end it was different, it was—" His face clouded over, but it was a momentary
cloud, with no storm in sight. "Except just before he died.
The same exact cantatas and Brandenburg concertos if he
had married twice, as he did, or remained single, like Master Handel—or our friend Abel. As for me, I do not doubt
his love, but my existence meant not a whit of difference

for his art or his inspiration. He kept everything—even the death of his own father—at a distance. So sensual and yet so far away. Whereas you . . ."

"Whereas I . . . ?"

"Nothing. Just a passing thought. That everything does affect you. That this conversation we are holding will someday find a peculiar, perhaps subterranean, path into something you are writing—and that very idea, that this is how you compose, it's . . . comforting. Comforting, but also disturbing." He stopped for a second. "I would give all my operas for the chance to be able to inhabit your head, just for a short intermezzo, just to catch a glimpse, merely to satisfy my curiosity. And then, of course, withdraw. But I suspect that once we go into somebody else's mind, there is no turning back, you're a prisoner there forever. So, all in all, I'll just linger inside my own small self, not risk that sort of adventure. It is enough to have your music, that you have so generously shared with me. You do leave me, however, with a problem."

I did not respond, confident that he would now say something that would allow me to advance Jack Taylor's suit.

"My problem is that I do not have anything to bestow upon you in return," Bach continued. "No pieces I have composed lately, excellent as they undoubtedly are, approach yours in daring and melodic imagination."

He had said it, he had, he had, he was creating the opportunity I had prayed for. I pounced. Not really pounced. More like slid my foot in the door so he could not close it.

"There are other ways of repaying favors, Maestro. There are things you might do for me that are not necessarily musical."

"Name it, my friend. Anything. You have but to name it."

I named it. I pronounced the word *Jack* and then the word *Taylor*. And hastened to tell my mentor that his erstwhile adversary had served and saved me during the harsh test fate had sent, how I would have succumbed to despair when it seized me by the throat, how the son of the Chevalier had healed me into sanity, emboldened me to complete the piece he had just praised so lavishly, that we owed such a wonder to that loathsome man's company. "It is not much that he asks," I concluded. "Just a few minutes of your time."

Predictably, Bach frowned. He did not like this. Not just my springing Jack Taylor on him without warning. Not just the fact that this very Taylor had been lying in wait for him in Paris for two months. Not just that this oculist had been preying on a susceptible, devastated young man who had lost his mother and whose fortunes had dimmed. Worse than all this was that his pupil, his protégé, his little Wolfgang, had grown into this conniving adult, had buttered up his mentor with the aria and the sonata, had laid a musical trap for him, had employed music for a purpose so low and indecent, had exploited the most divine instrument God can give, like singing a song of infinite love and loveliness to a whore in order to get her to discount the prices of her services.

ALLEGRO

Johann Christian Bach felt used, used and abused and misused, and this was more excruciating and shameful than the prospect of any interview with any eye surgeon, no matter how murderous the father. Bach's eyes were saying it all. *How could you do this to me? How could you do this to yourself?*

"It is out of love that I act," I cried out, desperate because he misunderstood me so grievously, desperate because his harsh judgment was also well deserved. "This meeting I wish to arrange will not only be good for him, for this new friend who has been so loyal to me. Also good, I think, Master, friend, Christel, I am sure, for you. He says you know something you have not revealed. He says it is eating you up, has been coiling, like a serpent in a garden, inside you for nearly thirty years. He says it is your last chance to face the truth. And I believe him—at least, his sincerity, I believe he sincerely believes this to be so."

"What last chance? What serpent?"

There was more alarm than anger in Bach's voice and demeanor.

I pressed on: "He will not tell me, will only tell you, tell you if I am present to guarantee that there will be no trouble. He dropped only one hint. He said: 'Tell the honorable Johann Christian Bach that I know about the letter.'"

"The letter? What letter?"

"The letter to Handel, he says. He says that his father, the Chevalier, told him before he died about a certain letter. Jack Taylor would divulge no more to me, sanctioned me to lay this secret before you. He adds that he has no interest in anyone else in the world knowing about that letter nor what it contained nor what went on that night that the Chevalier talked alone with your father in Leipzig, that night you yourself told me about in London."

"And what does this matter to you? Why should you involve yourself impudently in affairs that do not concern you, that occurred six years before you were born?"

I could have answered that any matter concerning my mentor should matter to me, that it would be dishonorable to desert a friend such as Jack Taylor when he was in need. I could have answered that I was old enough to judge for myself what interested me. But I would not have been telling the whole truth.

"The truth," I said, "is that I have become obsessed. I think something happened to your father and perhaps to Handel, just before they died, something special."

"What happened to them? What happens to every man, what will soon happen to me and then someday later to you, what is so special about this case that you should risk everything, our friendship and my esteem for you, to provoke me, to force me into an encounter I have strenuously avoided for so many years?"

I told him.

Blindness, I told him.

When I had been a child in London I had not yet experienced, could not even conceive, in my innocence, what blindness might mean. But two years later, in Olmutz, when I was eleven, the vermin of smallpox had crawled into me

and for ten days I was more dead than alive. For ten days I
had lost my sight. Those had been the most horrible days of
my existence until then, would be until the recent death of
my mother. What was horrible was not that I could not see,
but that this darkness was, in a twisted way, a relief. That
is what I told Johann Christian Bach: I had kept composing in my head, had even dictated, in my delirium, notes to
my father, who had never left my bedside. And that what I
had composed had been better than anything that had come
before and maybe anything that I would create afterward.
When I had emerged from the fog of that sickness and recovered my vision, the first thing I did once I had looked
myself in the mirror and discovered my face disfigured by
the pox was to tear up the sheets of music compiled during
those ten days, destroy all proof of the sublime summit I had
reached. That is what I told Johann Christian Bach: that I
detest the scars that will always mark my features, but also
welcome them as a reminder that someday perhaps I will
again sink into the crater of blindness and find those notes
waiting for me there, on the other side of the night, perhaps
the face of God.

"The face of God? Again, the face of God?"

He began pacing up and down the room, stopped at the
clavier, sounded five dissonant notes.

"So all this is about blindness, you say?"

"I think I have something, Christel, to learn from your
father. I think we both do. I think you should speak to Jack
Taylor."

We met, the three of us, the next day, early in the afternoon, on neutral ground. They were both staying at the Hotel de Bretagne but I decided something in the open air would be more conducive to smoother sailing. There was a café I particularly liked—and to which I tried to steer anyone who was willing to invite me and shell out thalers for the bill—on the Isle St. Louis, just on the tip, facing the gardens and the back of Notre-Dame de Paris and the waters swirling past it.

I had reserved a table outside and, arriving earlier than either of them, had placed three chairs, a perfect triangle for what would, I presumed, be a civilized conversation.

Jack Taylor was, as usual, loitering nearby—who knows how long he had been gawking around for my presence to authorize his—and I sat him to my left. He stood almost immediately, nervous and pale and as close to sick from anxiety as any man could be. I indicated that he should settle himself down. He did, but rose right away as the portly figure and awkward gait of Johann Christian had heaved into view from the Rive Droite direction.

I also stood up, and both of us, Jack and I, bowed simultaneously, like singers or actors after a performance, except that the performance had not begun yet, I could only hope that we would all bow as graciously and amicably when it was over.

Johann Christian did not offer to shake hands.

He installed himself at my right.

I made the unnecessary introductions as best I could, stuttering with false gaiety that they had not met but that their fathers had and that therefore—but I swiftly choked back my words and signaled to the proprietress to bring us our coffee.

Each of my friends waited a bit—perhaps for the other to start, perhaps as a way of finally sizing up their opponent, remark if he was as grand or as small as time and mythmaking had devised, neither of them willing to believe that this was actually occurring, neither of them ready to make his move till the other acted first, until, as if animated by an invisible clockmaker or a distant puppeteer and ventriloquist, they both uttered the same peremptory, parallel word.

"So," said Johann Christian Bach, at the same time as Jack Taylor verbalized his own "So," and then both lapsed into another round of obstinate silence.

I broke the ice.

"Mr. Jack Taylor has something to convey to you, Master Bach, and hopes that, after he is done, you will, in turn, have something to reveal to him. Perhaps it is up to the one who sought this conference to open the proceedings."

Jack nodded.

He explained that his father, the Chevalier—and Bach snorted at this title, at the fact that John Taylor Senior had baptized himself with a nobility and pedigree no king had conferred upon him, but Jack ignored the snort, made it irrelevant by what came next: that his father had died six years ago, in this very city. That before expiring he had made to his only son a confession and that it was this confession that Jack Taylor now wanted to report, word for word, as far as was possible, to Herr Bach.

"And this confession deals with the death of my father?"

Jack Taylor nodded again, grateful that the coffee arrived just then, distracting our attention, giving him time to subdue the turmoil he must have been feeling.

"I have only one request, Monsieur Bach. That no matter how arduous you may find my revelations—or rather, those of my father—that you do your utmost not to interrupt me or abandon these premises. No matter how detestable the Chevalier may be to you and your family—and this afternoon will elucidate whether that hatred is grounded in reality—his deathbed words deserve respect. Can we have, on this matter at the very least, a gentleman's agreement?"

It was Johann Christian's turn to nod. Though several times during the next hours I saw him fidget, several times caught him biting his lip, several times noticed his legs tense and feet arch up as if to take flight, he did not interfere once, suppressed every sign of derision or incredulity, while Jack Taylor deployed his remarkable story.

The beginning was similar to what Christel himself had laid out to me thirteen years earlier. The Chevalier's arrival in Leipzig in March 1750, his lecture at the city's concert hall attended by every illustrious and high-ranking citizen, his first successful operation on the elderly Bach, a relapse into blindness more complete than before, the urgent request for the Oculist to visit the ailing Kapellmeister in his quarters at the ThomasSchule.

"They shut themselves away"—Jack Taylor now entered a part of the story that Christian had not witnessed—"for two hours, my father said. He said nobody else had been present and that nobody else, save Handel, ever learned what went on in that room, though he did imply that possibly one other person, namely yourself, Maestro Bach, might have some inkling as to what had transpired."

Jack Taylor stopped, as if he was concerned that Johann Christian would forsake his vow of silence at this suggestion, would vigorously deny any such inkling or clue or even notion, and rise from his seat and terminate the interview. It was almost as if Jack Taylor, having reached his long-delayed goal, and advanced to the edge of the cliff he was about to jump off, wanted to give himself one more chance to back away, give Christel the chance not to jump into the abyss with him.

But the London Bach kept his promise as well as his temper, staring at both of us with a stone face, not giving even a sigh permission to escape his mouth. He listened to the story of his father's last days as if they did not involve him, as if they had befallen somebody he hardly knew.

Johann Sebastian Bach had, as soon as he had ascertained that the door was firmly closed and locked, sworn the Chevalier to secrecy. It was a request the Chevalier was used to, that he had complied with on many an occasion and had no problem consenting to now, "as long, sir," he added, "as this does not damage my honor." The elder Bach assured him that there was nothing dishonorable in what he was about to propose. On the contrary, it derived from a transcendent desire, even if it might appear at first glance—and here, the sightless composer had smiled at the irony of the phrase, uttered by a blind man to an eye surgeon—a bit odd and unorthodox.

"I have spent my life, sir," the elder Bach had said, choosing each word with deliberation, like a distinctive note on the organ being struck clear as crystal. "I have spent, I say, every conscious moment of my existence in the service of God. I might go so far as to declare that I have wagered my immortal soul on the certainty that my music has been the best way of glorifying His name. As I composed and as I played the organ and as I performed my sacred works—and those that did not seem sacred but still contained enough loveliness to please our Lord—I often felt transported into His Presence. With all modesty, my minor creativity was a way of imitating His incessant creation and sustenance of everything. With all modesty, I was merely following in His footsteps."

The Chevalier had interpolated at this point a comment of his own. "We are not that different, you and I, musicians and doctors. An artist tries to give form to a misshapen world, and a doctor tries to give health to a deformed and infirm body. Competing not really against others who practice our art or even against our own imperfections, but against death. Knowing that we are going to lose that wager. But music, I must acknowledge, dear Kapellmeister, can go further than medicine in this struggle for healing. If I have done my utmost to restore your defective sight and would do so again a second and a third time, it is so you may continue your heavenly work. That is my task: to ward off dissolution so that ordinary mortals can, through you, touch a piece of Paradise. I am an artist of bodies who saves lives so that an artist of souls such as yourself can end up making our lives worth saving."

Jack Taylor paused. "That was the sort of man my father was, truly was."

Fearful that this would be too much for Christian, I hurried to throw in my own question. "And how did Johann Sebastian respond to this comparison?"

"I understand," the elder Bach had responded, "but I fear that you do not. Let me repeat that I have never been as close to God as in my music. And nonetheless, even in the most sublime moments, there has been—as inevitably for mortal men there must be, or so I thought—something missing. One tiny gap between myself and God. God was always one rapture away, God was always receding as I advanced in my fugues, one step ahead of me as I pursued Him, so near, so proximate, so immediately touchable, so prone to my embrace and yet sliding away into eternity even as I soared, God disappearing behind a cloud even as my sound and harmony enveloped, nay, stormed the sky. I could not admit that this was disappointing, as I knew that the distance was the distance of death, that I had to cross that river to reach the Throne of Heaven, that only then would a true fusion with God be possible. I told myself that I needs be patient and wait for Him beyond the gates of Paradise and beyond the gates of my flesh. Then I would see Him

in all His Magnificence. But even so, as I grew older, as my
days became numbered, my end looming, I begged God for
one instant of reprieve and certitude, that He should allow
this servant one glimmer of His Aura, one nuptial instant
of melting into His Arms. With my own eyes, that is what
I pleaded for—let it be with my mortal eyes, just once, just
once, before death ushered me across the threshold where
only the inner eyes of the soul would reward my thirst."

Jack Taylor ceased speaking here for a minute or so.

We all looked at a barge that was slowly navigating the
Seine in the warm, drowsy afternoon. It did not seem possible to me that Johann Sebastian Bach had ever pronounced
words such as the ones the Chevalier had attributed to him
or that they could be recalled by his son with such eloquent
precision. But then, nothing seemed real to me in that interlude, all, all of it, my two friends, the stones of Notre-Dame,
the flow of the river and the birds, my own existence, a mere
dream, Christian's inexpressive face, my fingers drumming
the underside of my chair, Jack's stirring of his coffee. He
took a sip, realized he had not put any sugar in it, served
himself a generous spoonful, then another sprinkle, tasted it
again, smacked his lips with satisfaction.

I tried to concentrate on the Chevalier's last moments
in this very city, bidding farewell to everything that my own
eyes were feasting on, tried to think of Bach in his Leipzig
quarters, who could not use his eyes at all. I wondered if
Jack Taylor was also hearkening back to those two—or was
he doing nothing more ordinary than taking a break and

enjoying the taste and aroma of the coffee that proved that he and his tongue and throat were so, so alive. As regards Johann Christian, it was useless to try to guess what he might be thinking. He sat there, as unmovable as the cathedral towering on the horizon, as unmovable and more difficult to decipher.

I was jolted out of my meditation by the voice of Jack Taylor, by the voice of Johann Sebastian Bach resurrected on the banks of the Seine, thanks to the unsolicited mediation of the Chevalier.

"I begged the Lord for this sign of His Favor," Christel's father had supposedly said on that evening twenty-eight years ago. "And the Lord answered me. He brought me you, Chevalier John Taylor, as his instrument. He sent you to me to fulfill His Design for this lost member of his flock seeking to safely graze. I did not know this when I agreed to have you operate on me. I thought that was merely a way of recovering my sight so I could continue my service, my musical pursuit of eternity. But I was wrong. I realized how wrong I was when the operation was successful. At first, of course, jubilation! I assumed I had been awarded many additional days, months, years of life and creativity. And yet, along with the new light to my eyes there came also a visitation of distance. It was as if God had grown quiet, had vanished. I had felt so close to Him when I was blind, when my physical lens had been closed to the colors and contours of the world, making His Presence under the guise of sound and love all the more precious and immediate. The flood of light you brought back into my existence was a curse, Chevalier Taylor, it was separating me from the light inside, it was denying me the one thing I desired before I perished, the one glance at God that would confirm His Benevolence. I realized that God wanted me blind, wanted me to sacrifice my human eyes, wanted me to enter the eclipse of darkness, the blankness that lingers and remains on the dark side of the moon and the other side of the stars, so that He could approach me."

I gasped at these words, but neither Christian nor Jack seemed to hear me, so immersed was one in telling, the other in listening.

"The thought," Johann Sebastian Bach had said, according to the Chevalier Taylor, "was so arrogant, so sacrilegious, that I dismissed it, I fled from its implications. Who was I to interpret God's actions and intentions in this way? What sort of sinful creature takes it upon himself to gouge out the eyes, windows to the soul, that God has bestowed upon him, who was I to dare and presume that I had been chosen as one who might meet Him, as our Savior did, while still remaining flesh? Did I claim that my music had made me as God incarnate, Incarnatus Est, how I could even conceive of such a blasphemous notion? Was it not Satan who was leading me down this forked path, befouled with fog and confusion? Or was it no more than the delirium of old age, a hallucination of the sort that befalls men to compensate them and make easier their passage through the valley of Death?"

Jack Taylor looked now at the London Bach and then at me, as if seeking encouragement or perhaps forgiveness for even entertaining such thoughts, for being the messenger. I remembered my own blindness, those ten days of agony, and realized with horror that I could recognize and make mine this madness, could identify with someone who might indeed wish to be plunged into darkness, and trembled all the more at the idea, because that was where Jack Taylor's story, that was where the Chevalier's confession, that was the chasm where Johann Sebastian Bach's words, were inexorably leading.

"I want to make sure," the elder Bach had continued, "that your second operation, Chevalier, is a failure. I want to make sure that when the bandages are stripped off, I will see no more. I want to make sure that this pitch night you will summon me to will be interrupted only once, for a few hours. That is what I require: that I be blind, totally blind, save for one flicker of relief before the curtain finally draws to a close forever. So that in that moment I may again penetrate the nebulae that hide the face of God."

"Even if it means that it may hasten your own death?" the Chevalier had cried out, aghast, according to his son, at what was being demanded of him.

"Especially if it brings on my death, dear Chevalier. It is the price God exacts for admitting me into His Presence. Can you, awarded every degree from every University, honored by every sovereign from Moscow to Lisbon, can you guarantee this? Not the skills of any common butcher, any ephemeral quack, any of those false surgeons who can divest us of our vision with the fell stroke of a lancet. But the skills of the true physician, a musician of healing, who so controls the mysteries of the eye as I control the mysteries of song and sound, that he may erase vision and then bring it back and then steal it away again, like a magician, like God Himself. It is that interval I seek, those limited hours when the world will return to me in all its multiplicity, so that I may measure how paltry is what I see with my orbs compared with what I am seeing as inward man, the full Face and Unity of God revealed to me in the dark. Can you accomplish this?"

Jack looked at Christian, reached out a hand toward him, did not touch even his sleeve, but it was as if the Chevalier in person was speaking directly both to the father in Leipzig and to the son in Paris.

"I will be reviled," Jack Taylor said. "That is what my father answered. He knew, he knew. That it would be said of him that he blinded the great Sebastian, that he would be called a murderer, that he would be hounded with insults and injuries. He asked your father to relent, oh, that was not a task that he accepted willingly."

I could hear him, I could hear the Chevalier at the tip of the Isle St. Louis as if he were still alive.

"Why should I do something so contrary to my calling," cried out John Taylor, Eye Surgeon and Oculist to His Majesty George II, "such a betrayal of the Hippocratic oath, why should I engage in such black practices, having sworn to do as little harm as possible? Why?"

"Because it will be your greatest operation, your greatest achievement, even if it remains a secret between you and me, me and God, God and you, because only the three of us know, will ever know."

"That's not enough," and here Jack Taylor's voice rose, breathless, as he impersonated his dead father, what his dead father had said to the dead father of Johann Christian Bach, what nobody could confirm or deny ever on this earth because there was no turning back the crowded course of time, "not enough," the Chevalier had insisted. "You may be content that this stay a secret, but I have many decades yet to subsist and it is a heavy burden for me to carry, a vilification that will pursue me beyond the grave and haunt the legacy I leave to my son, my only son."

"It cannot be known," replied the elder Bach, implacably. "What I am doing, what I am planning, this scheme of mine to stand before God's Throne in my own finite, melting flesh, that is something my wife cannot know. It would kill Anna Magdalena, to think that I deprived her of years of my comforting love, have left her bereft and impoverished, that this dereliction was deliberate on my part, that I should care for this quest of mine to see God more than for her well-being and the future of my sons, and above all, the care of my poor daughter Regina Susanna and the other girls, that I should ruin all their lives so that blindness may deliver a final glorious lesson, no, it would be intolerable for my family to know."

"Intolerable for them to know, but not intolerable for you to do it, suffer them to suffer so?"

"It must be so. I must do it and they must not know."

Jack Taylor winced. He avoided looking at Johann Christian Bach, fully aware of the torment he was inflicting upon him in spite of the express orders to hide this story. Jack could not bear to continue, he could not bear to and yet did, he continued what he now might be repenting of having started.

"They sat thus, for a long while," he said, "the grand musician and the grand doctor, they sat, unspeaking, for more minutes than the Chevalier could count. Your father needed this kept a secret, Herr Bach, and my father needed it revealed, and there seemed to be no possibility of a compromise that satisfied the otherworldly desires of one and the worldly reputation of the other. Finally, Johann Sebastian Bach spoke and spoke but one word."

Jack Taylor paused and I knew the name he was about to pronounce and so did Christian, we both heard it ahead of its being pronounced, all three of us let it float in our minds like an echo from that frozen night so many years ago in London.

"Handel," Johann Sebastian Bach said.

The Chevalier asked him what the devil did he mean?

"Handel," repeated the elder Bach. "I will inform Handel about our agreement. I will even suggest that he follow my lead, so he may also, as a true Lutheran, avail himself one day of your services. That is what I can offer you, Chevalier."

"And you are expecting Handel in Leipzig? Because I do not think you will ever travel again after the fateful operation you have stipulated."

"A letter will do. I cannot write in my own hand any-more, but I can dictate it. And then have it delivered."

"Me? You want me to deliver it? You are demanding too much, sir. I am expected in Berlin and—"

Jack Taylor smiled at the absurdity of the situation, and, to my astonishment, Christian smiled back—or at least shared in the joke. Whether he believed this to be a true dialogue or the product of the Chevalier's imagination—or of his son's—was not clear to me, but it was encouraging to see him make an effort to participate instead of sitting there like a wall.

The elder Bach had also laughed. "No, of course not," he had responded. "Somebody else. One of my sons. Christian, I will get young Christian to deliver a letter of vindication personally to Handel. That is the only way to prevent it from being lost, my assuming full responsibility for placing it in his hands. And thus, if anyone was ever to doubt your efficacy or your goodness or besmirch your reputation—but why should they?—you could then point them tactfully to Handel and he would provide proof, or at least confirmation, that you acted under my instructions and under protest. Will that be sufficient, sir?"

And his father, Jack Taylor said as tears began to glisten in his own eyes, "my father, out of the kindness of his heart, said yes, he would do it. He kept his part of the bargain, Herr Bach. Now it is up to you to keep your part."

He settled back in his chair.

The afternoon was ebbing toward its end. A child passed by playing with a hoop, round and round it went, round and round. A pair of lovers stopped in the shade of a tree just off the embankment of the river to whisper something to each other. The sound of a horse furiously galloping on the Rive Droite reached us.

"Are you done?" asked Johann Christian Bach.

"I am," Jack Taylor answered. "I have been true to my father's name and true also to your own blessed father, sir, with the hope that he is in the heaven he so desired to see. And I thank you for your forbearance, as I thank Master Mozart for having the courage to bring us together. I am relieved by this encounter, Herr Bach, and trust you are as well."

"Relieved, is that the word you used?" said Christel. He kept his voice low, barely above a whisper, and there was no sharpness, only a minor modulation in his voice, but there was no mistaking the danger bubbling under the surface of such sensitive politeness. If anything, the hoarseness in his throat was frightening. Anything could happen. I had seen him erupt before and feared that, despite his initial courteous tone, we might be in for another bout, except that this time the object of his rage would be present and ready to respond, as any man would, to a provocation or an affront. There was no longer a child between them acting as an intermediary, no longer someone whose innocence could mandate a truce. My innocence had died the day my mother had left this earth, perhaps the evening when I had sunk to my knees and asked the Virgin to intervene and save her, and received no response. I could no longer believe that there would always be a good outcome to my pleas for redress. On the contrary, I suspected that I might have occasioned, with my meddling, a deeper and more violent split between these two adversaries than when they had sat down on either side of me in the shadow of Notre-Dame de Paris. It would not be the first time in my life when my best intentions led to disastrous results.

No, no. Bach was keeping his temper, on this occasion something other than mere good manners was holding him back.

"Relieved, so you're relieved?" he repeated. "Well, good for you. If you believe this irrational, preposterous story, good for you. If that is what you need to sleep at night, having had such a monster and a liar for a father. Not only did he infect mine, blind him permanently, occasioning his death, but, not content with these crimes, he wishes to erase his ineptitude, concocting this outlandish, profane tale and, mark my words, does so only when he is no longer around to be interrogated regarding its many contradictions and flagrant absurdities. Your father expected me to swallow this grotesque befouling of my father's life, his last days? He expected, you expect, that I will condone this picture of my father as blasphemous, as self-destructive, as a man who would sacrifice the happiness of his family for a crazed, quixotic quest for a God he has faithfully, even stolidly as the Lutheran that he was, served his whole life? Your Chevalier expected me, you expect me, to believe that the greatest musician of his time and perhaps of all time—as future generations shall someday acknowledge—would connive in a pact with such a quack, such a fraud, a man who would prance into a town and operate on ten men with cataracts and three squinty-eyed women and collect his substantial fees and then flee before they realized that they had been cheated and were now worse off than before? You expect me to deem this—this claptrap—to be worthy of the slightest trust?"

This entire diatribe had been pronounced, I insist, very quietly, without a hint of irritation, almost dispassionately, almost as if Christian felt these were accusations he had perforce to recite because someone—his father, his mother, his absent sisters and brothers—was expecting that sort of defense. Was that what accounted for the monotony of his harangue? That he was merely playing out his assigned role as dutiful son, and therefore restraining himself, not exploding righteously, as he might have if something had not been bothering him, yes, something was definitely curtailing his indignation.

And if I could observe it, so could Jack Taylor. He did not answer the invective, he did not insist on the unimpeachable morality of his father, he did not challenge the London Bach to a duel or anything that silly. He merely said, after a pause so long that in the stillness of the afternoon it almost seemed as if Christian's words of infamy had not been uttered, Jack Taylor merely asked:

"So there is no letter?"

"What letter?"

"The letter to Handel."

There was alarm, even panic, in my mentor's eyes, even as he responded oh so gently: "Look, I understand that you wish to respect your father's memory, I understand that what the Chevalier said as he lay dying is sacred to you. I respect that, I truly do. A son who stands up for his father, no matter what that father has done, I doff my hat to such loyalty. But you must equally understand then that I must just as steadfastly stand by my father, defend his honor against calumny."

The weakening of Johann Christian's attack on the Chevalier invigorated Jack Taylor.

"So there was no letter?"

My mentor stood up.

"I think, sir, we have come to the end of this conversation. I have fulfilled my obligation to Master Mozart, and there is no more to be said."

Jack Taylor did not move.

"Just swear to me that there was no letter to Handel, swear to me on your father's eternal soul, may he rest in peace, swear to me that you did not deliver that letter, and I will leave this table and never trouble you again. Why is it so difficult for you to simply answer my question. Again: Was there a letter to Handel?"

And now it was the turn of Johann Christian Bach to be relieved, now it was his turn to harken back to the year 1750, when his father had died and his own fortune had changed forever.

My dear mentor, shuddering with emotion, sat down in his chair again and, for the first time in the afternoon that was lapsing into evening, looked straight into Jack Taylor's eyes.

"Yes," said the son of Johann Sebastian Bach, "yes, I delivered that letter to Handel."

We waited for more, Jack Taylor and I, we let the seconds tick by, and when enough time had limped away and my mentor remained obdurately silent, then, for the second time that afternoon, I interposed myself into the conversation.

"Then you must tell us," I said to the man who had taught me so much, who had rescued me on a snow-laden day, who had welcomed me into his life and music with such generosity, who was ready to forgive me for having surpassed him, "dear Christel, you must tell Jack Taylor all that you know, so the truth may finally shine."

"The truth? The truth? That it may finally shine. Ha! You have not grown at all, Wolfgang, you are still a child after all. You really believe that the truth shines, that it will ever shine, as in a fairy tale, that we can ever know what happened in the past, in men's hearts?"

He was wrong about me. I was mature enough not to respond to his imputations. I pronounced not a word in my defense. Of course, I wouldn't have been able to anyway, as Christian charged forward with an avalanche of words, oblivious of the present company, speaking as if to himself or to his father or perhaps to the long-gone Chevalier, pouring out the story he had concealed for almost three decades.

"That I delivered the letter, that much is true. As to what it contained or whether it confirms or belies what the Chevalier confessed, ah, that is an altogether different matter, of that each of us must be the judge. This much I can verily attest to: my father's last blind days, in the weeks that followed John Taylor's second operation, were full of foreboding. Though he seemed more at peace than I have ever seen him, he also seemed inhabited by a sadness that—or maybe the sadness was mine and therefore colors my recollection.

"I was, at any rate, steeped in sorrow when he summoned me to his side some days before he died. It was, I recall, right after he had spoken to my sister Regina Susanna. And just as I entered the room, I saw Archdeacon Wolle, my father's friend and confessor, arrive behind me, ready to administer the sacrament. But first it was my turn to be alone with him.

"He clasped my hand in two of his—and his two were robust and my solitary one was trembling. 'My boy,' he said, 'I am dying. No, you cannot deny it as I cannot. You must be strong because my death will only be the start of your travails, and not the worst part. I have been through the death of a father at an earlier age than yours, at nine I lost my mother too, so I have some knowledge of what it means. I only wish my own father had spoken to me as I am now blessed to be able to speak to you. I only wish he had asked me to alleviate and soothe his last moments. Are you ready to do my bidding?'"

Christian sighed. "I told him anything, anything he wanted, anything at all. He indicated a letter that was on a table next to his bed. I knew that it existed because he had spent the previous day dictating something to his assistant, Bammler, behind closed doors. I had been beset, I admit, by pangs of envy. I did not comprehend why I was not being favored for what was evidently an important task. Had he not preferred me as his secretary, was I not aware of all his other correspondence in those days? I had even mentioned this to him when he had demanded the solitary presence of Bammler in his bedchamber. He shooed me away. 'Oh, you are too young to be burdened by an old man's final, brooding thoughts. A time will come for that, when your soul will be prepared to read my soul. But meanwhile, I will have need of your services for something far more transcendent and onerous than scribbling last-minute messages.' And the next day he made good on his promise when he asked me to pick up that letter sitting on his night table.

"It was sealed, and fat with many pages. He wanted me to take it to Handel. 'I have reports that he is in Halle these days, visiting his birthplace. It should not take you long to go there—it is but thirty miles away. You will be back in time, my boy, to say good-bye.'

"I told him that I could not leave him, not knowing if ever I would see him again. What if Herr Handel was not in Halle or had left for some other destination? 'Then you must follow him.' And he persevered with this thought: 'You must follow him to the ends of the earth if need be. My honor depends on it. Do not let this letter out of your sight until it is conveyed unto his very self. No servant, no promises from a footman or a mistress or an innkeeper, no assurances from a friend. Handel, and no one else.'

"When I protested that this enterprise could well take months, he relented and agreed to let me set out after his funeral and once his will and testament had been opened. And added that I must swear on the Bible that I would not read the contents of the letter nor ask Handel to reveal them. This latter instruction riled me. My father was entrusting me with such a delicate mission but did not feel I was old or wise enough, at fourteen, to share whatever solemn message he wished me to carry to Handel. Nor was I happy about abandoning mother and sisters in their bereavement, when they would have most need of my solace. And all of this to convey a letter to a perfect stranger, a man who had shown no interest ever in meeting my father?"

My mentor shook his head, as if trying to clear that memory. It would not go away. He was suddenly overcome with emotion, as had happened so often to Jack and me during that momentous afternoon. He controlled his feelings by veering onto a slightly different subject.

"Perhaps it is worth explaining this—this relationship, or lack thereof, between my father and Handel, in spite of my dear friend Abel's insistence that they were most intimate. What is true is that they were born forty miles from each other, Handel in Halle and my father in Eisenach, the town that also witnessed Luther's birth, a divine sign of happy coincidence, as Johann Sebastian was fond of recalling. But more significant was that the two greatest musicians of their time came into this world merely a month apart from each other, Handel in February, my father in March of 1685. My father never ceased making efforts to see the composer he thought was his superior—an interest that was never corresponded by the more famous but, let me state this without reservations, less endowed Handel. When my father was thirty-four years old and Kapellmeister at Coethen he heard that Handel had journeyed from London to visit his mother in Halle and immediately trekked the scant thirty miles to see him. For naught. Handel had departed a few hours before my father's arrival. Was he aware that my father was on his way, and did not wait? We will never know. But we can guess. Because ten years after that mis-encounter between the two composers, Handel, now even more famous, was again in Halle to see his mother, Dorothea, I seem to recall her name was, like that of one of my sisters. My father was in Leipzig by then and, ill with fever, was unable to make the journey. He asked my brother Wilhelm Friedeman to seek out Handel and invite him to Leipzig. It was only twenty miles away—the distance between them kept getting shorter, forty and then thirty and finally twenty miles, as they grew older—but once more, Handel did not cooperate. He sent back his regrets. Despite this rebuff, the very next year, on hearing of the death of Handel's mother, my father traveled to Halle to attend her funeral. He wrote to Handel on that occasion, he told me once, detailing the ceremony in the hope that this might alleviate the pangs of her passing away. Receiving no answer, and always ready to think the best of his fellow men, he assumed that the letter had been lost. Nor did Handel come to call on him when my father was blind for three months, nor when he was on his deathbed. And this was the man for whom I was to forsake my home?

"My father always had the gift of musical divination but also was able to divine the thoughts of others. He answered mine before I formulated them. 'Poor lad,' he said, 'you have no home. Soon enough you will leave your mother and your sisters to fend for themselves as best they may.' I remonstrated with him, reminding him that I would be back in Leipzig after completing the mission he was charging me with. 'But then you must go and seek protection and guidance under the roof of Carl Philipp Emanuel in Berlin. Your half brother will take care of you.' He then signaled that there were some ducats for me in a nearby chest, to sustain me during my upcoming voyage, no matter how long it might take.

"And he became oddly cheerful. There were things, he told me, that I would learn on this journey that I would be thankful for later in life, might even see his disappearance as a godsend that freed my spirit from yesteryear's bonds."

Johann Christian shifted his eyes toward me and away from Jack Taylor, who had been digesting this without a wink, as if he were a statue, afraid perhaps of breaking the enchantment of the moment, afraid that any interruption would stop these memories that seemed to confirm his father's own story. So he must have felt a reprieve when my mentor directed his gaze at me.

As if the words Johann Sebastian Bach had pronounced twenty-eight years ago were meant for me, for me when I was nine and alone at Dean Street without father or mother, for me now at twenty-two when my mother was dead and my father was far and my sister was irate, both of them blaming me for our dear Maman's demise, I felt those words from the past enter me mercilessly.

"My father said: 'It will be the first time you are on your own, that you must shift for yourself in a world that is not fair, where talent is rarely rewarded and evil abounds, Christel.'

"I answered, desperate: 'And you will not be there? You will not be there?'

"He smiled at this, as if to say that we are always without our parents, that we are all born orphans, that the lives of a father and a mother are merely on loan to us, and that we should never forget that all power and glory derive from God our Father, in whom we must put our trust so He will not disown us. 'I will soften the blow of our separation, my boy,' he said. 'I will leave you three harpsichords and a set of pedals. A determination of which I will apprise your mother, your brothers, and your godfather Graff. This bequest is above and beyond whatever shall be your part in my, alas, meager estate. These four instruments will provide some resources for you during your years in Berlin.'"

My mentor lifted four fingers and pointed them upward, gazed at them in wonder, as if they were the three harpsichords and the set of pedals rather than merely appendages on his hand.

"My father was in touch with God more than any other man I have ever met, but he also knew the appetites of men and the practicalities of everyday life, he knew that this ultimate enticement was something I would be hard put to resist. Oh, he did not doubt that I would have carried out whatever task he commanded anyway, but those harpsichords! Once I had accepted them, I could not go back on my promise to find Handel."

The sun had now dipped behind one of the towers of Notre-Dame, casting a blue haze on the river and the café and the two lovers who were still leaning against the tree as if they wanted to fold it into their bodies.

Christian shivered in the late-afternoon heat, still unrelenting in that month of August, he shivered as if it suddenly dawned on him what he had been relating, the story he had never told anyone before.

"But enough," he said now, "enough for one day. I am hungry and dinner calls and then an early bed. I am not recovered yet from the miserable drive from Calais."

He gestured to the proprietress to bring the bill. Jack immediately took out some coins. "Oh, no, Mr. Taylor. You and Wolfgang are my guests. I am no longer that lad of fourteen who was so hard up that a set of pedals seemed like a fortune."

Jack Taylor was resolute. "I was the one who insisted on this rendezvous, sir, so it is only reasonable that I play the host. And oculists such as myself, who have built a name for themselves, as you have in your own profession, are much in demand and therefore able to afford these trifles and many more."

For a while, they amiably fought over who would foot the bill. I did not offer to mediate, taking care of the matter myself. Mainly because I was in even worse financial straits than when Jack Taylor had approached me after the Concert Spirituel in June—I had lost even the three pupils who had supplemented my already negligible income, and my gambling had done away with another loan my father had sent my way—but also because an offer to resolve their dispute would have interrupted their good-natured bickering. Better that they should be struggling over a louis d'or than differing about what really might have happened on a remote night in Leipzig.

My prudence soon had its reward.

Jack Taylor was unable to wrest the bill from the claws of Johann Christian Bach. Unable to persuade my mentor to even accept a contribution to the afternoon's entertainment, Jack was able, however, to secure, on the other hand, a victory on a far more vital matter: he insisted that he reciprocate by taking us all out to dinner.

He knew a *traiteur* run by a Madame Minot who could rival the *restaurations* offered by Monsieur Boulanger on la rue St. Honoré—Madame Minot's was not far, right next to the Porte de St. Antoine. "Too much noise," I protested, though my mouth was already watering at the prospect of a second free repast in one day. Jack assured me that by the time we'd get there—less than half an hour's stroll—the demolition work of the day on the Porte would have been completed and we could enjoy a good meal, an excellent wine, and even better conversation.

"Some fried liver dumplings, eh, Master Mozart?"

"A ragout for me," Christel exclaimed.

"If you love ragout as much as I do," said Jack Taylor, "you will thank me eternally for taking you there."

On the way, I purposefully lagged behind in the twilight, let them give free rein to ordinary conversation, such as would animate any pair of old acquaintances. Not a mention of blindness or God, no comparison of music and medicine, no reference to fathers and sons, letters and fate. They dwelled upon friends they had in common, with Bach providing the latest tidbits of gossip from London (Samuel Smith deceased! No? Yes!—and the price of sugar—terrific news—had significantly diminished since a large shipment had sailed in from St. Kitts) and Taylor bringing Bach up-to-date regarding what Parisians were up to—Marie Antoinette, again pregnant—and then on to current affairs, how King Louis's siding with the Americans, his declaration of war against Britain, was depleting the treasury and affecting the price of bread. Both Bach and Taylor agreed (what a relief, that a war half the world away had not led to a falling-out between them just when they seemed to be settling their own private war) that it was folly to try to keep a people subjected to a power deemed foreign and oppressive. When they passed a little girl who was begging for some coppers in front of the Église Sainte Marie, they both gave her some alms and lamented so much misery, more than they had ever remarked in London. Jack Taylor ascribed this to good works ordinary citizens were able to accomplish, such as his own care for the poor and blind at Hatton Gardens,

and Christian replied by telling him about the benefit concerts he and Carl Friedrich Abel had organized for old and
impoverished musicians and invited him to attend one when
they were back in England, though this might have to wait
until Abel was over a fungal infection that had attacked him
after his recent rapid visit to Paris, and Jack wondered if he
might be of assistance, but was informed that it was not, alas,
of the eyes that Abel suffered but of a urinary disturbance and
burning, and Jack countered that such afflictions often had
consequences for the vision of the patient and he would be
glad to help, if such were the case. And then described some
of his most successful eye operations and Bach, not to be outdone regarding accomplishments and plans, outlined the plot
of his newest opera, where the protagonist, Amadis, must go
through several trials by fire, using song to conquer the heart
of his love, held captive by evil spirits. So that by the time we
stopped at the corner where la rue Jean Beausire starts, they
were so familiar with one another that nobody could have
guessed that these gentlemen had been acquainted a mere few
hours ago and at each other's throats, at that.

"Ah, Wolfgang," said Jack Taylor, turning to me as we
drew near his favorite *traiteur*, "in there," and he pointed at
the gloomy fortifications of La Bastille looming above us,
"my friend Dr. Alphonse Landru still languishes, with no
hope of quick release. They have confiscated every copy of
his pamphlet so no harm was actually done, in spite of which
they will not discharge him. And at least forty other gazet-
teers and scribblers rot away with him."

"Only petty men fear petty writings," I said.

Christian Bach looked at me with a mix of admiration and perplexity, as if seeing me for the first time.

"So, your ideas have grown along with your body, Wolfgang. I must take back the hasty words of reproach I addressed to you anon. While at the same time warning you, as mentor—or former mentor—that expressing such ideas with such abandon can be dangerous."

"Oh, that phrase does not belong to me. Nor to anyone real either. I borrowed it from a character in a play. Figaro, a barber, the sort that works often with practitioners such as Dr. Taylor."

Bach knew what I was talking about, that was on everyone's tongue. *The Barber of Seville*, a play that had not yet been staged in London.

"I heard those words at Madame d'Épinay's house near the Chateau de la Chevrette," I made haste to explain. "The author, Beaumarchais, was in attendance. He had written that phrase, precisely, that only petty men fear petty writings, for his character to utter but then, out of prudence, had removed it and several other protests against the abuse of power from the play. 'But I will reinstate them,' he promised, almost boasted to those present at the soirée. 'And I am working on another play, where Figaro marries—a sweet, sharp-witted girl called Susanna—and he shall have his say at the end and tyrants will tremble, I warrant you.'"

"Susanna," interjected Christian. "Like my sister. Though she never married. As far as I know, that is."

We looked at him with curiosity, awaiting further elaboration, but he changed the subject. "Your friend Beaumarchais had better watch out," he said, somberly, "or he will end up with Mirabeau in Vincennes. Or with our good Dr. Landru in there."

"He has good company with so many prostitutes," chortled Jack Taylor. "Not to mention lunatics and young aristocrats sequestered away by their fathers or husbands by their wives to avoid scandal. When the real scandal are the lettres de cachet. Ah, if the French but had our Magna Carta!"

By now, we had sat ourselves at a nice table that Madame Minot had selected for us, overlooking a quiet courtyard covered with flowers and wafting with delicious smells.

After we had placed our order, the conversation turned to other abuses of power, the suppression of the rights of assembly, and again to the foolish colonial wars of King George that were not going well at all. Whether Jack's concord with Christian on these and other matters was a mere tactic, a way of buttering up the son of Johann Sebastian in order to induce him to an even more amicable association, I could not tell, but the result of such political harmony, plus barrels—at least that's what they seemed by their abundance—of the best Burgundy, brought us to the point that, as the meal was winding down and we were being served a splendid *mousse au chocolat*, the London Bach was in a bright enough mood to proceed with his narration instead of returning to the hotel to rest, as had been his original intention.

This decision to tell the rest of the story had come at my prompting. When he had declared how wearisome these journeys were without the cheerful company of his dear Abel, and how he pined to be back in London in the arms of his wife, Cecilia Grassi, I used the opportunity to suggest that in his youth he must have seen the road of which he now complained so bitterly, with its ruts and poor food and rheumatic dangers, as a fabulous adventure. Had his quest for Handel been the first time he had traveled?

"The first time," Christian said. "And it was arduous, let me tell you, though it might well qualify as an adventure." He sighed and quaffed down some more wine. "Because, of course, Handel was not in Halle, had come by for only one day to kneel at his mother's tomb and then disappeared without a trace. I spent several days in search of the slightest clue as to his whereabouts, and finally the choirmaster of the church, who was not a great enthusiast of Handel's music (too many pagan themes, he said, too many promiscuous biblical stories) or of Handel himself (what sort of son takes twenty years to pay his respects to his dead mother?), reluctantly revealed that this man who had been so ungrateful with his native town had headed north to Aachen to take the waters, though who knew if that was the real reason for voyaging to that dissolute metropolis. Off I went, then, to Aix-la-Chapelle, as I still prefer to call it.

"I had never seen anything like that imperial city, with its enormous cathedral built by Charlemagne so he could be crowned Emperor—and yet I was more impressed by its bustling streets, crammed with visitors who seemed more interested in the array of warm, wanton women than in the heat of its natural springs. I had never seen so many men afflicted by syphilis, so many deformed faces. I was glad that Handel was not there so I did not have to remain one more hour than necessary. I soon ascertained that he had indeed spent some time at a nearby spa—his health had been failing, they told me—but had left several weeks earlier, apparently to the nearby Netherlands.

"I tracked him down, town by town, city by city, all the way to The Hague. By this point, the ducats were dwindling and I began to fear that my father's injunction to follow Handel to the ends of the earth might turn out to be literally true. Bad news greeted me in that majestic city. Meneer Handel had been injured a week before—late August that must have been—in an accident. The carriage had overturned on the appalling road to Haarlem. Rushing to the latter city, afraid that I would be unable to deliver my father's letter at all, save to a corpse, I was informed that the great composer had recovered enough to be moved to Deventer, where he was the guest of Royale Princess Anne, a friend of his and daughter of George II. I sped there, to that lovely town where Erasmus had been schooled—so many spires and churches, such a wonderful promenade next to the Overijssel, reminding me of my now faraway Leipzig. I arrived there on September fifth, the day of my fifteenth birthday, and deemed this a sign that my mission would soon be complete."

Christian let out a long, a prolonged puff of breath, so protracted and persistent that I marveled that anything was left in his lungs.

"I need to stretch my legs," he said. "Let us walk back to our hotel and conclude this story and this affair in that chamber they set aside for us yesterday, Master Mozart. It is a more fitting place than this *traiteur*, no matter how regally they have treated us. I have some liqueur, a few cigars, that will help us end our session in a pleasurable way."

He was right. More hungry patrons were pouring into the premises, the rowdier ones boasting of having just sampled wine from a nearby cellar, there were two thousand bottles waiting to be imbibed, one was drunk and amiable enough to lumber over and invite us to come back with them if we didn't believe him. I peered behind the reeling man and noticed, there, at his table, the very same wide-bosomed redhead who had amply embraced Carl Friedrich Abel at the fancy whorehouse I had refused to enter. She winked her eye at me suggestively, perhaps soon she would saunter over and offer her services. Oh yes, it made sense to retreat to a refuge that guaranteed us more privacy. Jack Taylor paid the bill and we stepped out into the night of Paris, bid farewell to the swaggering Monsieur Réveillon and the dreadful walls of La Bastille, and set out across the Faubourg St. Antoine.

On the way to the Hotel Bretagne, not one of us uttered a sound.

As soon as we had settled in the room—the piano was still there, and various other instruments lay close by, a welcoming reminder to me that I had not yet exhibited all my latest work to my mentor—Johann Christian Bach launched back into his tale, as if we had not been interrupted by our lengthy Parisian walk.

"Weary as I was from over a month of continual travel and hardship, I made my way to the palace where Princess Anne had decided to retire after the end of her regency. A footman answered the door and, after one scurrilous look at me, demanded that I go to the back entrance. I explained that I was not a servant but a musician and had traveled a long way in order to deliver a letter to Master Handel. As my father had anticipated, the lackey proposed that I hand the letter over so he could place it in the hands of Her Royal Highness's guest. I refused. My instructions were explicit. We were at an impasse when the voice of a woman floated toward us, asking about the visitor. Daring the wrath of the footman, I answered the invisible interlocutor with my name and added that of my dead father and his charge to me. 'Oh, Bach.' The lady's voice quivered and ordered the retainer to step aside.

"It was the Princess Royale herself. She had heard of my father from Handel, she said. Handel himself was under the weather and resting, though much better from his quite serious accident. But she would be glad to listen to me play something for her—and if she was pleased, she would invite me to partake of some refreshment and stay the night. And then tomorrow I could speak to her friend Handel, if he was so disposed.

"I did not tell her that if Handel was indisposed or, more drastically, simply not disposed to meet up with me, I would then have to camp outside her palace until he was ready, that I had not come so far to be frustrated in my undertaking. Such a determination on my part turned out to be superfluous. I played some of the later, more complicated pieces from my father's *Art of the Fugue*, inching toward the soft cadences of the Contrapunctus XIV—do you remember it, Master Mozart, the one you played for our merry company after we supped at Dean Street?—that he had been working on, perfecting, perfecting, always striving for perfection, at the time of his death. And there I was, reaching the conclusion, adrift in its harmonies, tears streaming from my eyes as I remembered that father I would never see again, his eyes that would never open again, those words of his, *So be it*, when he had last looked out onto the Leipzig sky, there I was, transported, forgetful of Deventer and the Princess and the palace and the road that brought me there, when I was resurrected to my own body and fingers by the intuition that there was somebody other than my hostess listening to me. I plunged on into the dark, polyphonic dissonance of the multiple themes interwoven by my father and, having reached the final tactile moment of his pursuit of eternity, I stopped, my hand suspended in midair, I stopped because there were no more notes to play, I stopped because my father was dead and there was nothing I could do about it, I stopped because I knew that when I turned, George Frideric Handel would be there.

"He was standing at the door. And though radiant at what he had just heard, there was also a terror and sorrow in his face that I had not expected.

"He cried out, 'So he is dead! Your father is dead! He must be dead if he sends one of his sons here, such a young lad, such a fine and strapping lad. And so talented. Bravo, my boy, bravo! I was sleeping upstairs and in my dreams I thought I had died and was in heaven and when I awoke I was still in heaven because the music continued. But why did you stop?'

"I rose and bowed. 'Because he is with us no more, as you guessed, sir. This was his last fugue, and he did not complete it. But he did send me with a message for you, only for your ears, if you are indeed, as I hope, the great Handel.'

"He came over to greet me. He was a portly man, flush-cheeked, with a large, shining dome of a forehead and sensual lips, perhaps a bit thin for so broad a face and yet cherub pink. There were no signs of his recent accident or convalescence, though when he clasped my hand, I noticed his was weak and sweating, and he immediately had to sit himself down next to Princess Anne. 'So yet again, we have missed each other. I will have to wait until the two of us play for our Lord. Which may be soon, sooner than I ever expected, for I am not well, I was not well when the devil of a carriage overturned and now am much worse. My eyes, my eyes.'

"Our hostess stood up. She would order a bed to be made up for me and a bracing dinner, which she hoped might revive me so we could engage in some conversation that might be to my benefit. And then she was gone, attentively leaving us alone so I could deliver my message.

"He received the envelope and opened it with care. I watched him read the forbidden letter my father had dictated, read it once and then all over again from the beginning.

"He was silent for a long time. So long that shadows began to invade that room.

"I was about to say something when the same unpleasant footman brought in some candles and placed them, flickering, near Handel and, without looking once at me, withdrew to some hellish den.

"Handel sighed, tapping the letter into his palm with the same slow rhythm of my father's counterpoint. 'How did he know,' he asked, 'how did Sebastian know that I would be ill, that my eyes would be failing?'

"I was surprised at the question. I had no idea, of course, what was in the letter, how it might have elicited such a query. I answered in the vaguest possible terms: 'He was always worried about your health, dear sir, and knowing that you were both the exact same age, and that you both engaged as youths in the same nocturnal reading, the same practice of music at the same stark and squinting hours, he may have presumed that you might be similarly afflicted. Dare I conjecture that he imparts some advice to you, perhaps a warning, Master Handel?'

"'He does, he does. But his letter is, well—exceedingly strange, exceedingly so. And from what I have heard, your father was not a man given to excesses.'

"'Save in his love of music, his devotion to his family and his pupils, and, of course, in his submission to the Will of God and the demands of Providence. In that he could be deemed excessive.'

"'Yes, yes, of course. Well, he invites me to join him, *join* I suppose is the right term, invites me to become his twin, he says. And I will treat his words with the seriousness they merit, I will think on them in the days and months to come, I will take them to heart if ever I have need.'

"And that was that."

We waited for Christian to continue. But nothing came. He closed his eyes and for an instant I imagined that he had fallen asleep. "That was that," he reiterated, his eyes still tightly fastened, as if with a lock. "There is no more."

"What do you mean?" Jack Taylor asked—anticipating what I myself wanted to ask. "How can there be no more? What was in the letter?"

Christian flung himself resignedly out of his armchair and walked to the piano, looked down at the keys, played one, then another of them meditatively.

"My father was right. That voyage changed my life. After dinner, that night, Princess Anne asked me to play for her and for Handel one of my own compositions. When I was done, she clapped her hands and said that once I had completed my studies in Berlin with my brother, I should visit London, where my talent might someday be more fully recognized than in the provincial towns of Germany, thus following in the footsteps of Maestro Handel. 'What think you, George,' she said to him. 'Does he not show promise of a style gallant, unlike the heaviness of his father, no matter how much we may appreciate that form of polyphony?' Handel responded that there was a place for everything in music but that he believed I would prosper in London, to look him up if he was still alive and he would lend some sustenance. Princess Anne interjected that I should dedicate myself to operas, this was where the future lay for musicians. I said that my father had warned me to beware the twisted serpent of opera. He had not been partial to such pastimes, and I was not sure I would be any good at them. 'Then you must go to Italy, young man,' said Princess Anne. 'You must contact Father Martini and dedicate yourself to the drama and coloratura of the opera and reap the rewards.' How odd, eh? How everything turned out as they predicted that night long ago in Deventer. Why, I even have an Italian wife!"

Jack Taylor looked at me as if requesting my permission to persist in the question that the London Bach had so conveniently ignored. I nodded. I wanted to know the response as much—well, not as much, almost as much—as he did.

"The letter, dear friend Bach. The letter. What was in it?"

Christian turned to us, and I guessed the answer before he gave it.

"I don't know, Jack Taylor. I don't know what was in that damn letter, that blessed letter. Handel thanked me for my efforts, folded it back into the envelope, and left the room. When we sat down to dinner, he did not mention it again.

Nor did so the next day when I bid him adieu and he re-iterated that I would be loved in London if ever I spread my wings there. I returned to Leipzig—Handel paid for my coach—and we never saw each other again."

Jack Taylor had grown pale with each passing word.

"How can you not know what was in the letter? How can you have led me this far and deny this knowledge?"

"Handel did not tell me and I did not ask, following my father's very meticulous instructions."

"Well, no matter. Your story confirms everything the Chevalier confessed: that there was a letter, that you were to be its emissary, that Handel was to be informed of the pact. He knew, my father knew all these details. How could he have known all this, you, Handel, the letter, if it was not true?"

Christian gently interrupted Jack Taylor's parade of evidence.

"I'm sorry, my friend. But none of what you allude to constitutes proof, real proof. My father could have mentioned, en passant, that he would recommend the Chevalier's distinguished services to Handel—after all, when they talked that night in Leipzig he thought the second operation would be successful."

"Then why did he write to Handel when the operation failed?"

"Maybe it was to warn him. Maybe it was on some other, entirely unrelated matter. Maybe it was to get him to listen to the final fugue. Maybe it was to tell him that he was waiting for him on the other side of death, where they would ultimately play together in the court of the Lord, reveal to Him and to themselves the true musical operation of the universe. Maybe the Chevalier found out about the letter when he treated Handel eight years later—when he blinded him as well. Maybe on that occasion your father spoke to Handel of other musicians he had cured, like the Leipzig Bach, and Handel confided that he had received a letter from that very Bach delivered by his son Christian. Maybe the Chevalier saw the chance to use that circumstance to brew and concoct this tall tale, maybe he deluded himself into believing he was indeed innocent."

"Maybe, maybe, maybe! All of this is mere speculation on your part, Kapellmeister Bach."

"As is your story, Dr. Taylor. Neither of us knows the facts, that is the only truth. Neither of us was in that room that night in Leipzig. There was no third witness, nobody like our young Wolfgang, who has listened so attentively to your version and my version and may judge which of us is right. We are left, sir, where we were when all this began, as I knew it would all end when I refused to meet you. I did not lead you on. You were the one who insisted on this encounter. I accepted thanks to Master Mozart's insistence, despite my certainty that our altercation would clarify nothing. Each of us has remained in exactly the same position we occupied before we exchanged our respective accounts. Each of us believed something this morning and believes the very thing tonight. I know my father would never have blinded himself deliberately, commit such a sin against God. He loved life and his family, loved and respected his Savior too much, was too nigh to his death to risk everything, his damnation, on such a sacrilege. And you know your father, you say you know him—and no one will convince you that he was a charlatan, a bungler, a man who lived by his wits more than by his hands, a man who preyed on the candor and despair of the afflicted. I commend you for your faith in the Chevalier. And also thank you for having forced me to tell this story of my father's death and the letter I delivered to Handel, lifting thus this burden from my shoulders."

"You thank me, you—why then, did you refuse to meet me—or my father—during so many years if now you thank me?"

"I confess that I feared that you had some evidence, some real and hard evidence, that would sully my father's reputation, that would undermine my faith in him. I feared that the contents of that letter might be somehow damning. It is a natural fear. Demons make us doubt the righteous, lead us into temptation. But that fear can now be dismissed. My conscience is calm. I did everything I could to alleviate your pain and satisfy your curiosity. And there is nothing more to say."

Jack Taylor drank in these words as if they were poison. Then he nodded and stood up. There was a crazed look on his face, of a kind I had not contemplated before, not once in the two months we had spent together, certainly not the night he approached me at the concert in London or the next morrow in the freezing square.

"I bid you good-bye then, sir."

Bach bowed ceremoniously. "I trust that if we were to meet again, socially, in London, you will not touch upon this subject."

The glimmer in Jack's eyes was all the more maniacal because it was belied by the serenity with which he pronounced the next words: "I am not returning to London, Herr Bach. Tomorrow I leave for Leipzig."

"Leipzig?"

"Someone there must know. This Bammerl you mention, who took the dictation—"

"It's a fool's errand. Bammerl no longer lives in Leipzig. He is demented, lost his reason years ago. Even if you were to track him down in who knows what small town in Germany, you will not extract from his mouth more than nonsensical babblings."

"Then your mother, she is sure to—"

"My mother is dead, has been dead for seventeen years."

"Then your sisters, you mentioned your—"

"They know nothing. What can they possibly know? Or my two brothers. Leave them alone. You promised that if I met with you, that if I admitted the existence of that letter, you would be discreet about this affair, that you would be content. I have done more than you asked, allowed a stranger into my heart, my family's story, my father's demise."

Bach turned to me.

"Mozart? You have brought this man into my life twice. And are witness and guarantor of the pact we subscribed. I demand that you now make him obey the terms of that agreement."

It was the moment I had been fearing since Jack Taylor had sidled toward me that night in Carlisle House. The moment when I would have to choose between them. I did not hesitate.

"The terms are clear, Jack. You must not pursue this matter further."

"The terms are clear and I shall scrupulously observe them. Herr Bach will never be disturbed by my presence ever again. But our unwritten contract said nothing about being forced to abandon my quest for the truth. He says I should be content. For that, it would have been enough for him to have tonight confirmed that the letter did indeed indicate my father's innocence. I would have desisted from any and all investigations. As it is, I cannot rest until someone somewhere says, quite simply, yes, the Chevalier did not wrong the great Johann Sebastian Bach. When that moment of affirmation comes, as it must if there is justice in this world—perhaps in Leipzig, perhaps elsewhere—I will not trumpet that revelation, would never dream of using it to malign the Bach name. I need to know the absolute truth for myself and myself only. But it is a need that will not brook being denied."

He walked to the door, as if on the verge of leaving immediately, and then turned back into the room, drew closer to Bach and me.

"I thank you both for your indulgence. I wish you well with your Paris opera, Kapellmeister Bach. May your protagonist use song indeed to conquer evil. It saddens me that under other circumstances, we would have been good friends and spent many a merry moment in each other's company. As for you, dear Wolfgang, I wish you a safe return to Salzburg. May you someday find a city and perhaps a world and a time when your genius is truly appreciated, and your kindness finds its just reward."

He bowed solemnly, with an uncharacteristic stiffness, and left the room.

We were both quiet, Christel and I, for a long while.

"So, young man," said Johann Christian Bach. "What do you think?"

He was still at the piano.

I pointed to it.

"I think the answer is always music, I think we must always seek answers there when we are most lost, most bereft. You have brought your violin with you, I see. Let us play the newest of my recent domestic pieces, a sonata. You at the clavier, myself on the violin, let us see what it tells us."

It told us that everything is uncertain in life except pain and beauty. It told us that we are always, till we breathe our last, masters of our own fate. It told us that the only real sin is to add even one more sliver of sorrow to a world already overflowing with loss. No more sorrow than is absolutely necessary, that is what the Allegro told us, what the Minuetto that followed it told us. It told us that grief need not be eternal. It told us to believe that grief need not be eternal.

When we were done, when together we had been through the agitation and the quiet tempest and the brief moments of surcease and bliss, those all-too-brief moments of surcease and bliss, I embraced him. And whispered in his ear, so only he and the angels in heaven could hear me: "Go to his room and just say yes, just tell him that Handel mentioned something about the blindness of your father being deliberate, that you now remember that detail. Tell him old John Taylor was your father's instrument, not his executioner."

He whispered back: "He will not believe me."

"He will believe you because it is what he needs. Do it, Christel. Do it to give him peace and give yourself peace as well."

"Even if it is not true?"

For one more eternal instant, I was overcome with love for him, for Jack Taylor, for all the mothers of the world, for all the lovers who say good-bye in the hope of one day again saying hello.

I broke away from him, gently.

"I do not know what the truth is in this matter, Christel. But this I do know: we should help the dead to sleep."

"And the living," he said.

"And the living," I said, "while we can."

He remained there for what seemed an eternity, eyes closed, head bowed, as if praying or perhaps listening to the echo of our words, his words and mine.

And then left the room to do my bidding.

Alone in that room we had enchanted with the magic that had been born from my heartache, I realized that I had become the mentor and Christian my protégé, I realized that perhaps, after all, Jack Taylor had come to me for help a second time so God could teach me who I really was, force me to grow up.

What more to tell?

Bach came back and let me know that Jack Taylor had wept for joy and embraced him and sworn never to reveal their secret to anyone, not even to his own son. He would leave for London the next day with his heart full and his mind clear. He had sent me his fondest regards and to please consider his house mine if ever I did make it back to London.

As for Johann Christian Bach, I saw him a few times more before I departed for Salzburg some weeks later, precisely on his birthday, September 5, 1778. He was very busy with his opera, and I was trying to scratch up some money for the journey home to a bereaved father and an indignant sister and a greedy Archbishop, I was anticipating the looming day when I would have to choose between the two women I had fallen in love with, I was wondering if there was indeed one female soul and torso that contained them both and was awaiting me somewhere on this vast earth. And I was saying good-bye to the city where my mother was buried along with my hopes of fame and fortune.

I remember Christian now, when I last saw him with these eyes that have not failed me as they failed Bach and failed Handel, I remember him now, standing there, smiling at me as a father looks at a son who has done him proud, who has happily surpassed him. I see him now, so alive and full of delight, the last friend I visited in Paris before I left.

He died four years later.

Three years after that, Jack Taylor joined him in death.

Neither of them crossed my path ever again.

Only in my dreams can I see them now.

EPILOGUE

Leipzig, May 17, 1789

Requiem and Fugue

I am back in Leipzig again, again standing, for the last time, in the cemetery where Johann Sebastian Bach is buried.

Nobody is here but me and a hefty, ragged woman of uncertain age, whose face I cannot perceive, as she is bent over a nearby grave, digging out a stubborn weed and then garlanding the just-excavated scrabble of earth with a scattering of tiny flower petals.

At least she is doing something useful. Not like me. This second visit to Leipzig made no sense. I came only for a day, intending to return to Berlin to play for the Queen, as I must tomorrow, as I must if I am to have any hope of a post at the court, I came to this city for one day and stayed on eight more, waiting, waiting, waiting...My first time here, three weeks ago, I had already spoken to everyone who might hold the slightest clue to the mystery of the elder Bach's blindness—the questions that Jack Taylor would have posed in 1778 if he had not abstained from that journey thanks to Christian's benevolence. So it was absurd to waste still more hours asking and burrowing and raking leads that had been discarded during my first visit in April, all of them dead ends.

And yet I made the journey here anyway, postponing still further my return to Vienna, where Constanze awaits me with impatience and some irritation, as four of my letters have been lost. She must think I am infatuated with another woman, that I have escaped home in order to drown my despair in some singer's chubby arms. When all I wish is to return to my love, my dear wife, as I have written to her body and her soul this morning: *My little rascal cannot live without you, without seeking refuge in your nest, without your lovely bottom that I will spank many times as punishment for having doubted me, on that you may count.* And then, in order to cheer her up, told her how I speak to her portrait twice a day, once when I rise, once before going to sleep, and also, why not, of the concert five days ago at the Gewandhaus Theater. Magnificent praise, wild applause, invitations to dinner. But I lied to her about what really mattered, what she will ask about as soon as I walk through the door: hastily advertised and poorly attended, the profit I received was wretched—as I had cautioned Prince Karl, my newest admirer, but he insisted, he insisted and then asked if I could loan him a quick hundred gulden, and how could I refuse such a hearty fellow and traveling companion and brother Mason whose vows constrain him to acknowledge his debts? Though not immediately, as the next day he was gone in a flurry, leaving me with barely enough to pay for my keep at the inn, and nothing to take home to the tradesmen and creditors clamoring back in Vienna, certainly not enough to appease our hideous landlord who assails me each first of the month, demanding to be paid promptly—or the Mozart family will be cast out onto the street with whatever belongings have not been auctioned off.

And yet, and still, and yes, and no, I stayed on.

What am I doing here?

Why do I come back to this grave in Leipzig, each day at a different hour, as if that might provide a different response to the question that brought me here, that has been haunting me since my mother died, grown sharper when my father followed her into death in Salzburg, more agonizing as my own end approaches, mine, when I will no longer be here to tame the demons with my music, when the magic of flute and voice and clavichord will fail to protect me, will not even be able to fool me into believing that death is something that happens to everyone else and not to me.

The response is always silence.

Do I really expect Christel's father, gone these forty years, to cleanse my heart in this Leipzig cemetery, when my own father, when alive, did not provide an answer? Nor provided it from the other side of the grave, though I was not there to ask him when they lowered his body into the ground, have never visited his remains, never journey back to Salzburg, never will. Am I that mad, so estranged from everything I once loved, that I believe the dead Bach will deliver some message to me, some guidance, as he did to Handel? Give me the serenity that he found, the peace that eludes me?

A voice interrupts my thoughts, what was perhaps a prayer.

"He's here, you know," the voice says.

I turn.

It is the woman.

There is something familiar about her, the gesture with which she pats back a wayward string of graying hair, that full mouth, those jovial eyes, but where, when?

She thinks I am puzzled by something else.

"Bach. Johann Sebastian Bach. You do think you are paying homage to Bach, sir, way over there. It's what everybody comes here to do."

She stands up now. She is tall and plump, her clothes humble but her demeanor full of cheer—close to fifty years of age, though the deprivations she has been through make her look older. There is something doll-like about her face and body. Perhaps that is why I find her somehow familiar. Did Nannerl have a doll with this woman's round face, rosy cheeks? Nannerl, whom I have not seen for many years, whose wedding I did not attend, whose sons, Leopold and Wolfgang, I have yet to gather into my arms, my nephews, do they have a doll like this woman, did I have a doll like her, have I forgotten the days when I would sit with my sister and we would play with her dolls in our secret childhood kingdom?

No, it's not that. This woman's voice, something in this woman's voice.

"That's all right, sir," she says now, mistaking the twinge of regret in my face for confusion or embarrassment. "They all make the same blunder. The canons tell each visitor, there he is, measure six steps south from the corner of St. John's. At first I thought it was because they wanted him all to themselves, to not share him with anyone, but it's really that they don't know. They weren't there at the funeral, eh? Don't know a fart from the ass it comes from. Ha! Just like you, maybe."

I laugh. For the first time since I left Vienna and my Constanze, I give a hearty laugh. I like this saucy woman!

"I'm Mozart," I say, as if with that she'll understand that it's fine for her to make that sort of joke at my expense, everybody knows that I love a good joke, the smellier the better.

"Who?"

"Mozart," I repeat, now a little miffed.

"Mozart?"

"Wolfgang Amadeus Mozart. The musician."

She laughs again, throws a clod of dirt in my direction. I jump to the side to avoid it. I scuffle for a piece of earth and send it her way. She is very lithe for such a plump woman and escapes it effortlessly. Again that laugh!

"Of course you're the musician! What other Mozart would you be?"

"But you—"

"I just wanted to see your face when I didn't recognize your name. There are people, you know, who don't have the slightest idea who you are. I pass by people like that in the street every day. I hide among people like that, ignorant fools, knaves who don't know their heads from their butts, couldn't tell why a cantata isn't a concertino. At any rate, I'm pleased to meet you. I've been expecting you for a long time. He said someone like you might come. Someone worthy."

Is she also mad, crazier than even I am? I instinctively take a step back, stumble against a headstone. Right myself by grabbing hold of another.

She is delighted at my clumsiness.

"I'm not going to bite you, you know. Still got all my teeth—well, most of them—but they're not for taking a bite out of anybody. Not for chewing much food, either, ha! So you can come closer. Pay your respects. Here's where. Though it makes no difference to him where you stand, where anybody stands, what anybody does anymore."

Again, she laughs. Again, it is full-throated, joyous and celebratory.

I skip over several tombstones and two graves and find myself by her side, nimble as a child.

Because I know who she is, must be. But which one, which one?

Just to tease her, however—now it was my turn to have some fun—I ask:

"You can't possibly know where the great Sebastian Bach is buried. A peasant like you."

She sinks down on her knees. Gives the moist soil a tap with one hand while the other one tries fruitlessly to keep that strand of hair back, away from her eyes.

"Oh, I'm a peasant. Aren't we all? But not every peasant girl has been plowing this little plot of land every day of her life, sir. Well, since I was eight years old, since my father died. First with my mother for ten years and then...Not a day has passed that I have not knelt here, for I loved him dearly and he loved me, or so he said. And God has paid me back for taking such virtuous care of the ground under which he lies next to my mother. Seeing my industry, they gave me the job of upkeeping these other plots, give them a thorough cleaning. Tidy, aren't they? You can see, good Master Mozart, not a weed, not a one, no moss on each mausoleum. And if you want a grand tour, if you want to find anyone, well, then come to me. I'm their guardian, their best friend, I know where all the bodies are buried, I make sure they are presentable. Tidy, indeed. Except for him."

She picks up a worm. It dangles, wriggling, from her fingers. She kisses it, then drops it lovingly to the ground.

"The worms," she says, "them, I leave alone. See this one, so tiny, so easy to crush, to forget. I don't bother him, not him, not his family. They're just doing God's work. Like good little peasants. Soon enough he or his offspring will have a chance to make my acquaintance once again, meet me one last time, greet my breasts with their little teeth and legs, turn my own thighs into something useful for the earth.

Like my father, I do not dread that day. But you, you do dread it, you are afraid, Wolfgang Amadeus Mozart, musician. A pity you did not meet my father."

"So you are…?"

"Regina Susanna Bach, sir, your most obedient servant. Only surviving daughter of Anna Maria Magdalena Bach. The last one. Dorothea's gone, and Elisabeth, and even Carolina. Only me left. Hey, you look as if you've seen a ghost. But I do exist." She lunges out, takes my hand. Hers is warm. I don't try to withdraw it. She seems to appreciate that. "Not a ghost. Not me, not you, if we can touch each other, Wolfgang—you don't mind if I call you Wolfgang, do you?"

I didn't mind at all.

"And how about if you bought me a mug of beer and a nice roast? I haven't eaten a morsel today. Not much yesterday either."

I agreed.

She gathers up her skirts and places some rusty gardening tools in a basket next to the remains of an array of wilted flowers.

"Did he mention me ever?"

"Who?"

"How should I know? How many of my brothers have you met? All of them? One? You must have met one at least. You're a musician, they're musicians, all four, no, five of them if we count poor Bernhard, you must have crossed paths with one of them. That's what musicians do, as if I didn't know. Spend all their days mooning over each other, praising each other, stealing from each other, lamenting how poor they are, each and every one. So, which brother?"

"Johann Christian."

"Ah, Christel, of course. I gave him that nickname, you know. Couldn't pronounce, as a baby, the whole damn convoluted thing—Johann, most of the men in my family are called Johann, Johann this and Johann that and Johann the other. So, Christel, huh? Did he mention me?"

"Once or twice," I say.

"More times than he came to visit, that's for sure. More times than any of them came to visit. Not me, not my sisters, not my mother. Did I mind at first? Yes. Did I expect a letter? Yes. Do I mind it now, expect anything now? Not at all. That's the truth. And the truth is what matters most, is it not? The truth, the truth! Isn't that what parents teach their children? Did your father, did your mother, not teach you that when you were just a bit bigger than that worm?"

Johann Sebastian's daughter! Why should I interrupt her litany? Let her speak her fill and then eat her fill, eat till no more food could be stuffed into her ample body, pay for her dinner as a small token of my love for her brother, my need for her father's advice. And she has no acrimony in her, not a hint of it, despite her hard life and abandonment, no bitterness at all.

"How could I be resentful?" she asks, as if she could read my thoughts, just like her brother, just like her brother. "How can I not be brimming with gratitude? I was brought up a free bird in a house that was like a dovecot, our lovely *Taubenhaus* fluttering with life, people swarming in and out. Busy as my father was, teaching, composing, revising, performing, fixing organs, taking in apprentices, recommending others as they left for new venues, he always, always had time for us, for me in particular, always a kind word for me."

I take a long route into the center of town—rather than straight into the Brühl neighborhood, we stroll through the gorgeous and elaborate public gardens along the Pleisse, the promenade that Christel once described to me, where he first fell in love with Nature, blushed at the first girl he ever lusted after—I take as much time as I can with this old maiden, so we do not arrive at my inn quickly, so she may chatter all she wants, so she may entertain me, the one person I have met on this journey who makes me sidestep my bleak contemplations. Go on, Susanna, go on—your cascade of words is just what I need!

And go on she did, with mounting glee.

"Come hither, my little queen, my Regina, my Hosanna, my Hosanna in excelsis—that's what he called me, all those names, come here to your old Papa's lap and fill my nights with sun, fill my days with the serenity of stars. Gloria, Gloria in excelsis, if ever there were a creature who came straight from the fountain of God who is pure music— that's what he'd say, and then start singing, oh, he had the most affectionate tenor—come and give me comfort, most beautiful of all my beauties, someday you'll sing in all the cathedrals of the land and empresses will swoon at your sounds, but don't tell the other girls, don't tell the boys, and above all don't tell your mother, this is our secret."

She punches my arm, as if the secret were between the two of us, and I punch her back, more moderately, for she is strong, this sister of Christel's, this furtive sister of Christel's. I can feel her invigorating me, as if I were a tree thirsty for rain, reminding me, returning me to my most insolent, playful, perpetual self, the Mozart I have missed for many months now, several years now.

"How could I," Susanna continues, "bemoan a life that such a father started? Or this later life, this afterlife, that I can dedicate to his memory, the blessing of such a life in his company, alive then, dead now, are we to abandon those we love just because they are gone and cannot respond, at least with human lips? What? Has my existence been that desolate? Did I not have visitors to my bed, were all my dawns cold and lonely? But you cannot tell the canons or the City Council or any of those fools, Master Mozart, this you must promise, or they will strip me of my only permanent job and then the graves will choke with weeds."

I promise, gladly promise to keep quiet, I love secrets and pacts and games.

"Not that I can deny having been penniless, we had to beg day by day, we shivered at night, my mother and my sisters and I, my brothers did not come, they did not write, they did not send for me, for us, they did not inquire after our health. Is he well?"

"Who?" I ask, though I know the brother she means. I can also ask who, I can also play with her.

"Christel? Is he well? Thriving, healthy, prosperous?"

I wonder if I should not comfort her with a big fat lie. That her brother could not be in better shape, tell her, in fact, that he had asked me to pass on his regards if I met her on my Leipzig tour, perhaps slip some coins into her pocket on his behalf. What better way to honor the memory of my mentor? But I sense that such duplicity would not sit well with her, would demean this woman in a way that she does not deserve. Lies are for rancorous women, and she is sweet. The times when I dreamt of being a knight in shining armor to every lady who crossed my path are over. Only Constanze, only Constanze needs to be saved, saved from the sort of penury this daughter of Bach is enduring because she was not provided for. I must provide, I must find strength to compose more and be more successful so nobody pities my Constanze as I now pity this Susanna.

I tell her that Christel is dead, seven years already. I try to soften the blow by recounting his kindness, how he rescued me from boredom and fed me sweets and treated me like a son.

"I also loved him well. But, ah, if I had been born with something hanging between my legs, I would have been given the sort of training and food and lodging that Christel received, that you received, Wolfgang. But I do not lament the life I led. Did God deprive me, as he did my father, of sight? Did my father deprive me of his kisses and his delight,

when I was little? If I had never met him, if he had died
the night I was born, the night before I was born, the night
after I was conceived, then, yes, perhaps I would have cause
to complain. But he called me little bird. He called me little bird and we sang to each other and I will be eternally
grateful."

I see an opportunity to steer the conversation toward
Johann Sebastian Bach. If she was so close to him, perhaps
she has some information about his blindness, about the
Chevalier, about the letter. Buoyed by her energy and exu-
berance, I had almost forgotten that I was looking for a final
clue that would unravel that enigma. I had been confident
that Leipzig would offer up a surprise and, well and well,
here it was.

"Little bird," I say. "I remember that Christel mentioned
at one memorable dinner that your mother loved birds, starlings I think they were, and that your father bought one for
her once."

She smiles broadly and is about to respond when an unforeseen event changes her mood.

We have arrived at the Three Swans and are greeted
at the door by Herr Martius the proprietor, a tall, enormous man with dainty hands and a mincing step. He
is now almost dancing with excitement. He looks at my
companion, nods his head as if he had predicted, told his
wife, who bobs up and down by his side, that yon petticoat
would eventually catch this Mozart fellow and make him
pay for a jolly meal and perhaps something else—but he is

on peaceable terms with Mistress Regina Susanna Bach, anyone who can pay the reckoning at his establishment is welcome, they have been neighbors for all his life and hers, and he is not here on this earth to judge those who stray and those who say they don't. And at any rate, the news just received cannot wait.

I ask if it is the horses, if he has finally found fresh horses so I can return to Berlin tomorrow. I had not pressed the matter till now, but feeling the potency return to my limbs and soul, I am ready to move on.

Yes, yes, he answers, that's taken care of but what matters is not that, not that at all. There has been a rebellion, he says, in Paris, a revolt in the Faubourg St. Antoine or Antonius or wherever, hundreds have been killed, including some members of the French Guard called in to restore order.

And the worst of it was, says Herr Martius as he shows us to our table—a secluded one, as I had demanded—that twenty thousand bottles of wine in some cellars have been destroyed, looted, stolen, oh, what grandees could he, Herr Martius, attract to his Three Swans Gasthof if he possessed a fair few of those vintage bottles. What can justify such pillaging, such upheaval, such fury?

My new friend Regina Susanna has listened to this news from Paris avidly, quietly for a change, but as soon as the innkeeper has disappeared, after leaving us with a chalkboard displaying the possible selections, she launches into a long tirade, uninterested in eating or chewing or digesting anything other than the men in power.

Her rage, totally unexpected, comes surging from inside some deep well of regret, threatening to engulf her and me and the murals brimming with fairy-tale pictures on the walls, intent on consuming every corner of the tavern area, like the fire that perhaps is consuming Paris right now, as she speaks.

"It is happening. Ah, before I die I will see it, they will be paid in their same currency, they will see that there is justice on earth and not only in heaven. I could always sniff it in the air, I can sense it begin to descend, the terrible swift sword of God, oh yes, they will be swept away, it has begun, thank sweet Jesus and His mother, it has begun."

She pauses to breathe down a gulp of air and, before I can get a word in sideways, speaks of Albrecht, the man she should have married, the one man she would have accepted a child from, a child she would have called Sebastian.

"They came to get him one morning, hauled him out of our bed to fight in their stupid war. Almost three decades ago, but I haven't forgotten. I had heard the news, we all had, of the latest battle, Prussians and Frenchies slaughtering each other as if they were not all sons of the same earth, as if they did not have ears to listen to celestial music and eyes to see the sun rise and hands to fondle the breasts of the women they loved. But not him, not my Albrecht. He limped all the way home, right up to my door, a few days after the battle. *I could stand it no longer to be far from you, my love. I almost wanted a bullet to find me, a bayonet to carve my guts out, my dearest lark, so it would stop the pain of your absence, the abscess of your distance.* What, you don't believe me? You don't believe I could inspire words like those? *If I am alive,* he said to me that night, *if I did not allow myself to be taken prisoner, it is only because I kept myself for you, I knew you would die without me."*

She wants to cry but I am sure she hasn't cried for many years, I am sure she will not cry now, I am sure she will get over this attack of rage and grief—the rage, the rage, it reminded me of Christian, how alike were brother and sister, after all—she will yield sometime soon to her high spirits. But I must be patient, just as I was with her brother, I must let the anger spend itself.

"But it wasn't true that I would die without him," she continues. "He is dead and I still rise in the morning, eat what I can and when I can, clear the graves of my parents and sisters and neighbors, I am horribly alive. When I visited him in that jail the day before his execution, he told me not to be sad. *I was dying anyway,* he said, *and we spent one more night together—and is it not better to die for love than to live in solitude?* Such pretty words, he had a way with words, my Albrecht, like the men in my family had a way with sounds, but all his words could not save him, all the notes in the world could not save my father when his time had come, all the words he said and I remember cannot resurrect him. The one thing I cannot forgive. My brothers? All they have done is neglect me and my mother and sisters, which is their right, which is what men do when they leave home for other horizons, when they latch on to other families, other loves, other ambitions. Have you not done the same, Wolfgang?"

She doesn't appear to notice that I do not respond. "But the others, the ones who condemned my Albrecht to death...I went to see them—but did not weep, not like you, Wolfgang, you're the sort that cries, I knew it as soon as I lay eyes on you, mourning at the wrong tomb, ha!, but not me—I did not weep when I told them that I was to blame, I had bewitched him, I said. They laughed. You? You bewitched him? Get thee gone, wench, before we order a good dozen of lashes on your bare behind."

She seems faraway now, transfixed, transported, her frenzy slowly ebbing as she recalls her lost lover.

"I saw him. I saw my Albrecht swinging there, his trousers soiled, they put him there for me to see, so the whole town could see him. So this is what I pray. Not that they be hanged. The ax, the ax! That they survive for one instant after the ax has fallen, alive for just a few seconds so they can feel the pain, know what it is to have their body separated from their heart, as I did, as I still do, their eyes still seeing the world in all its colors, as I do even if my love is dead, their ears still hearing the crowd in the marketplace, as I do, as I do, their skin still feeling, as I do, as I do, the eternal freshness of the breeze. May it be so."

She is calm now.

"So be it," she says. "So be it."

"Yes," I say. "Your father's favorite phrase, I think. So be it."

"Was it? He wrote it yes, amen, amen here and amen there and amen all the time. But say it? Never. So be it? Or maybe he did say it from time to time and I don't— When I hear Papa's voice, all I recollect is him calling me little bird. But we must eat, friend Wolfgang!"

She was again the woman who had enchanted me with her enthusiasm for life, she was ready to demolish a whole cow and then a boar and drink ten barrels of wine, all the bottles that had supposedly been looted in Paris. What a contagious vitality she had, this woman with all the odds against her!

We put in our order—as bountiful as Susanna's endless cheer, driving me to half call, half sing out to Herr Martius, my aria from my very own *Don Giovanni*, *Vivan le femmine, viva il buon vino, sostegno e gloria de l'umanità!, sostegno e gloria de l'umanità!*—and only then, after toasting women and the glory of wine, did I return to the same question I had volunteered before news from Paris had driven her into reminiscences of worse times: "Little bird is a lovely way to refer to a daughter. If our little Theresia Maria Anna had lived more than six months, I would have called her so, but last year she—no matter, no matter. My wife is expecting again, and if it is a girl, then that will be her nickname. Our only son, my darling Karl Thomas, I cannot call him any sort of bird, he has no musical talent whatsoever!"

"Ah, may you be blessed with a girl. My father never regretted my birth. He'd sing whatever he'd been working on that day, my father, and then ask me to sing it back to him and that I did, his little bird, his starling. My mother loved starlings, though she could not afford to keep them once Papa died. And me? Well, I have not sung in all the cathedrals of the land, no empresses have swooned at my sound, have they? How could he have foreseen that his death would wrench my voice from inside me, mute my throat?"

Frau Martius had brought a large fowl of some sort—it seemed a chicken, but bigger—roasted to golden perfection, and wafting aromatic. Susanna let it simmer on the table. I did not touch it either.

"They brought me to his room, to say good-bye. *Kiss your Papa on the forehead one last time.* I did not move from the threshold. My mother's hands gripped my shoulders. She gave me a slight push. I stood halfway to the bed, mesmerized. He was breathing with such difficulty, gasping, wheezing, each breath as if it came from my throat and not his. Stifling us both, his life and my sounds, his heart and my future songs. Mama pushed me harder. She was stronger than me. I drew even closer to my father. He opened his eyes. He could not see me, of course, he could not see the drained, frightened face of his little bird, but he knew it was me, because he smiled. *Have you come to sing it to me, my little bird, have you come to help me on my last journey?*

"But I had not. I knew what he was murmuring about. All the others in that room were in the dark, more blind than my father was. A few days before, just before he had taken Holy Communion, he had summoned me to his bedside, demanded that everybody else leave us alone. He had clasped me close, sat me by his side and began to sing. Just like that, without an explanation.

"A heavenly melody, so serene.

"I began to cry. Back then I would cry often and easily, when tears had no real meaning. *Do not cry, little bird*, he had said to me. *It is the* Et Incarnatus Est *and you must sing it to me when I next ask you. Can you do that for your dear Papa?*

"I said yes, I would, but when the occasion came some days later and he reminded me on his deathbed of my promise, I was paralyzed. I was losing my voice, I was descending into terror, my throat was dying along with my father, falling in love, as his body was, with the emptiness with no name. He was dying, you understand, and I could not return to him the one thing he most needed from me, that I had promised to sing when he asked for it.

"He had given me the sheet with the music he had dictated to Johann Adam Franck. The last song, that *Et Incarnatus Est*, he had ever composed, offered it to me so I could practice it, study and rehearse and be ready, ease him with it into eternity, take it with him, my voice and his song joined for all time.

"I failed him."

It was time to intervene.

"Or maybe not," I say. "Maybe he understood that this was the greatest homage you could pay him, to lose your voice out of love for him."

"To sacrifice my life, yes, maybe. Because he smiled at me, my Papa, he smiled at me and said it did not matter, some other day, for some other soul in need.

"I had other plans. I spoke to God. *If You take him, God, I will never sing again. Let him breathe freely and my voice will return with each breath he takes. A few more years, Merciful God, a few more*

years not that much to ask, so I may grow enough, so he can prepare me
for the fate that my Papa has willed for his little bird.

"My prayers were not answered. My Papa died and I
never sang again. Knowing that, with my silence, I am betraying everything my Papa, severe and passionate, believed
in and created. Taking care of his grave when I could be
singing his celestial music and the music of others all across
Europe, your works, why not?"

"And you never repented, never thought, now it's time,
it's never too late?"

Now she smiles and attacks the food with relish. Gravy
dribbling from her mouth, she says: "Only once. When I
heard about a child of eight, my age when I lost Papa, I
heard about a child from Salzburg who was carrying out
the destiny my father had prophesied for me. I thought, this
may be a sign. If he can do it, so can I. It's never too late. But
by then I had lost my Albrecht, I had other reasons for not
singing, not for them, not for those who would feast while a
man like him is hung in the public square. But I did dream,
I did dream, Wolfgang, of the day when we would meet.
My father had said it would happen. Someone will come,
someone who is worthy, my little bird. Though it take forty
years, you will not be alone, that day you will not be alone.
That man, you can trust that man."

"Do you still have it?" I ask.

"What?"

"The *Et Incarnatus Est*. Do you still have it?"

I remembered what Christel had told me, about this
piece of the B-Minor Mass disappearing. It would be

fabulous to recuperate it, the body of Christ forged into a body of music.

"No," she says. "I burned it after they executed Albrecht. Burned it to cinders while his body was still swinging from the gallows. So I would never be tempted to sing it or sing anything, not ever. God took my father, then my lover. The Son of God will not receive consolation from my lips. Let Him seek it from those His Father pampers."

"You're not afraid of such thoughts?"

She shakes her head. She will never sing again.

"Unless you find the right song."

There was no such song, she says.

That we shall see!

I will make amends for what her father's death stole from her, that's what I'll do. What sweeter way to pay back the kindness her brother had shown me, even if that brother had abandoned her, had shut the door of their shared home behind him and never once looked back? If my music could restore her voice, was not that worth the whole trip, was that not something to take back with me and nurture and bring to my Constanze, inspire what are left of my days, no matter how brief?

I still have the key to the Gewandhaus, the hall where I had practiced for my concert. Would she be willing, once dinner was done, to accompany me there?

Something magical awaits us.

There it is, an hour later, with my belly full and my heart pounding, here it is, the piano I need.

I sit myself down at it, as I did for her brother all those years ago in London, and then again in Paris, perhaps I am destined to play for the whole Bach family, though not for all 160 members of it, ha! Just for this one little Bach bird. Evoke for her a woman, alone in a garden, waiting in the dark. One of my favorite scenes from my most popular opera.

I sing faintly as I play. The moment had softly arrived, *gioa bella*, time to fall into the arms of that song, might the night assist my plans, what I had written for a character, a woman I had imagined calling to her lover as I wished my own Constanze to call to me. Come, come, do not delay, my *gioa bella*, come to me, come to me in this night, *la notte*, what I could now imagine this daughter of Bach might have sung to her Albrecht one night among the trees, while the moon had not yet arisen, while all was dark and quiet, so that the stream would murmur and the breezes might play, *idol mio*, my idol, *ben mio*, gladdening her heart and Constanze's heart and my character's heart with their whispering, my whispering in her ear, her whispering in my ear, as flowers were laughing because the grass was cool and her legs could be discerned slightly askew, tilted to one side and the other and arching back and forth to allow someone like me, someone like Albrecht, to come calling. My gift to this Leipzig Susanna because I had created another Susanna before I met her, an invented Susanna who was singing to her Figaro, what a wonder, what a coincidence, it was that Susanna and this Susanna and every Susanna who would fill her lover's hair with roses.

Regina Susanna Bach is obviously entranced, her lips slightly open, her body swelling. She asks, when the song had ebbed away like moonlight: "Who is she, the woman in the garden who sings this song?"

"Her name is Susanna, like yours," I say. "She is in an opera I wrote, *The Marriage of Figaro*. Would you not like me to leave this music with you, so you can someday sing it? Not to me. To yourself, to Albrecht. Or would you like me to repeat the song? Now, right now?"

Hoping, elated, that if I insisted on a second round she might take up the melody, fully expecting that this aria meant and not meant for her would return her voice to this earth, that her father under that earth might thank me for again hearing her sing.

Instead, she says: "It is beautiful indeed, Wolfgang, but not designed for someone like me. You wrote it for your true love, a darling who awaits you, I am sure, whose portrait you speak to at dawn and before you go to bed at night. Oh yes, I know, I know you do that. It is what I do with my true love. But I have no illusions that Albrecht can hear my song, not anymore."

"It was meant for you! Every song is meant for every man and woman alive, alive or dead. And in this case, surely, the fact that her name is Susanna is significant, a sign that you should sing again?"

She laughs, as good-natured and humorous as ever, as if echoing a bell ringing nearby, from a tower nearby.

"Do you think your Susanna is the only one, the first one, eh?"

Puzzlement shows on my face.

She responds with an even more perplexing riddle. "Oh, silly boy, why should someone else not have brought another Susanna and her song to me?"

"Another Susanna? Another song? Someone else?"

"Why not? A Susanna who bathes in the cool retreat of a stream, flowing with murmurs, under pines and under a mountain, bathing naked in the hot summer breeze, banishing every woe, aching for her husband, her Joachim."

"But that is—that is—"

"Not just that song. Another one as well from that very Susanna, foretelling terrible things that may happen to her, separate her from Joachim, slander and slurs upon her honor. Two songs from the mouth of yet another Susanna, given to me just as you now give me your aria. If I did not then sing those songs, why would I do so now?"

It was Handel! Handel's *Susanna*! How had she, where did she—? Impossible that Handel's oratorio had been heard in Leipzig, where the opera house did not perform oratorios. How, when, where?

She rolls her eyes, as if only an idiot like me could misunderstand what had happened. Those arias were a gift—a way of thanking her for services rendered, pleasure offered, an old man made content, if only for a night—Wolfgang Mozart was not the only musician to come bearing a Susanna song in his baggage.

"Who? Who was it?"

And as soon as she says the next word, just that one word, I realize that I had been right to journey to Leipzig,

that there was indeed a message from Johann Sebastian
Bach awaiting me here, but not from inside his grave, but
coming from deep inside the flesh of his flesh, as soon as I
heard who had brought her the gift of songs composed by
Handel, I knew, I knew, I remembered that night in Dean
Street and what had been said and that I had hardly regis-
tered, and wished only that Jack Taylor were here by my side
and Johann Christian, both of them alive, to hear along with
me that one word, that name.

"Abel," says Regina Susanna Bach. "Carl Friedrich
Abel passed through Leipzig five years ago, on his way to
Potsdam. He was drunk when he got here and even more
drunk when he left. We spent the night together. No shame
in admitting it. Ha! He wanted to make love to some member of the Bach family, preferably female—and I was glad
to oblige, glad for the company, glad for the four meals he
treated me to, glad to sip his stories. Such a hearty man, so
full of vigor—who would have thought he was sixty-some
years of age. I wonder what has become of him?"

"He died two years ago, upon his return to London,
Susanna."

"Is this your specialty? To haunt cemeteries? To bring
tidings of death? First my brother, then Abel, who will be
next?"

I feel like telling her that I would, that the next time
she heard my name it would be to mourn my passing, but
the desire to predict such dire news had evaporated, her in-
curable optimism had cornered and dismissed my somber

thoughts—they might resurface, tomorrow they would undoubtedly throttle me again, if another child of ours died, if
Constanze were so ill again, if, if, if, but for the moment they
had ceased to abide in me, those depressing thoughts, they
were straining away from me like a sewer after a storm—
and, besides, I am anxious to ask her about Handel. Could
this be, finally, the answer to the puzzle? Had Abel told her,
during that visit, about a meeting with Handel he had attended just before Handel's death?

"Not a word."

"Not a word?"

Again, she laughed. Teasing me. Of course Abel had
told her about that meeting—just after he had sung to her
the Susanna arias from Handel's work, not only to impress
her with time spent with such an illustrious composer but
also because her own father, Sebastian, had made a stellar
and surprising appearance in the tale.

I was breathless, hardly believing this stroke of luck, of
fate, of Providence. The dead, the dead. She would speak for
the dead, for Abel, for Handel, for Johann Sebastian Bach,
for Christel, for Jack Taylor, for all those who had something
to tell me from beyond the grave, the extraordinary chain of
voices that was bringing the story to me.

Because, in effect, Abel had been invited by Handel to
his Bracken Street address—Brook Street, I corrected her,
Brook Street. And as he waited downstairs to be admitted
to the chamber where the composer was sequestered, frail
and bedridden, Abel had made the acquaintance—alas,

briefly—of the young soprano Cassandra Frederick, who had been asked by Handel to come visiting that Thursday. Handel had sent her some music from the last oratorio he had written, *Jedediah? Joshua?*—*Jephtha*, I corrected her—*Jephtha*, yes, that was the name. Handel wanted to hear two passages from it, Cassandra explained. *He is in a bad way*, she had added. *He is sure he is about to die.*

Susanna wondered if I wanted so many details? As it concerned her father, she cherished every minute word Abel had told her, but perhaps I would rather jump to the end and...

"All of it," I said. "You cannot imagine how long I have waited to know every last element."

She shrugged her shoulders. She was used to the foibles of musicians, their obsessions with one another, she loved giving pleasure to others, she would not skimp on any facet of the story.

Cassandra had handed over to Abel the score of the music so he could verify that Handel had indeed chosen ill-omened arias. Abel's fears were confirmed when, a bit later, both he and Cassandra were escorted into Handel's presence. The blind composer was propped up with pillows, in a mood of deepest despondency, dejected, wan, and in the dark. He had brightened up when he heard Cassandra's voice, *Ah, you have come to bring me my own song, so that I may meditate and brood upon it. Come, my dear soprano, you must sing the lines for me, you must sing them as if the world is about to end, as it is, as it is indeed, for me—and you, Mr. Abel, you must then stay behind and give me your opinion, as if it came from your mentor, the Leipzig Bach, himself.*

Here, Susanna paused. "Have you heard this oratorio?"

I lied to her, I told her that I hadn't. Why burden her with the story of Jephtha, a father who sacrifices his daughter because of a promise made to God, why add to Susanna's pain? And might that not deter her from telling more about Abel's visit to Handel on his deathbed, what she was recounting even now?

Abel had been impressed, he had told Regina Susanna Bach, with the two passages from the oratorio that Cassandra had sung. The first was from the very beginning of *Jephtha*. That oratorio started off with the dramatic words *It must be so.* And Handel had nodded after hearing that line, asked her to repeat it and mouthed the words himself in unison, *It must be so, it must be so.* And then, *I wrote the music to those words. So true that I asked the librettist to repeat them several times throughout that oratorio. And now, the other passage, Cassandra, the other one.*

And the soprano had then sung, *How dark, O Lord, are thy decrees! All hid from mortal sight!*

Susanna pursed her lips, trying to remember. "The rest of it—something about joys turning into sorrow and triumphs into mourning. And the words *Whatever is, is right.*"

I could visualize the scene as Susanna described it, as transmitted by Abel to her.

Handel had waited for Cassandra to leave before turning to Abel and saying: *You know, I was composing the music to those lines, those very verses—all hid from mortal sight—when I lost my vision. My left eye, it collapsed, and my right one dimmed. So I could not continue. No more dawn tomorrow, tomorrow's dawn, I can no more. For ten days I waited, I waited for my sight to return of its own accord. And it did, my vision was restored without any medical intervention, and I knew that the Lord did not wish me to languish in eternal night, blindness was not to be my fate. He wanted me to complete Jephtha, it pleased Him that His warrior is ready to kill what is most precious to him, the apple of his eyes. That man is ready to bow down, as I do, as I did, like Job, to the Design of God. But that was the last time, young Abel, the last thing I ever really wrote. The eight years since then have been barren. I should have listened to him. I should have listened to your mentor, Johann Sebastian Bach.*

Abel wondered what Handel meant.

Bach had written a letter to him, Handel said, sent him a letter, an exceedingly strange one, that Handel had received some months after Bach's death.

"A letter?" I interrupted Susanna's story, so excited I could not contain myself. "What was in it?"

Abel had asked exactly the same question.

God had seen fit to join them at birth, so close in years, so close the cities where they had first seen the light, God would make them twins in the dark abyss of joy, unify us as if we were one if only you heed me. You need not fear blindness.

And what else?

Everything is song.

Susanna repeated those words her father had sent to Handel. *Everything is song.*

And then was silent. She, her father, Abel, Handel.

"And that's all?" I asked.

It was what Susanna had asked Abel, what Abel had asked Handel, what Handel searched in his memory to find in that message from Bach.

Only that, Handel had said. *Everything is song. That is all.*

"And he said nothing more, are you sure? About a warning? About seeing the face of God? Not a word about operations against blindness, about music and perfection?"

"Nothing."

"Nothing about the Chevalier? Not one word about the Chevalier?"

"What Chevalier?"

I did not tell her. Why open up the possibility that her father had deliberately hurt himself, abandoned her knowingly, the story that had beleaguered Christian?

Or maybe she would have responded, with that simple bluntness, straight to the point: "Does it matter, Wolfgang? Does it matter at all?"

Indeed, indeed. Did it matter? What had really happened that night between the Chevalier and the elder Bach? Whether the Eye Surgeon was a criminal and Bach was a saint, whether Taylor was the instrument of Bach or his executioner? The only two other men who had passionately cared were dead, and my own obsession was sickening me. Would it change anything in my future if I discovered that Jack Taylor had been telling the truth, that the blinding had been premeditated? Would it solve my problems if, on the contrary, Christian was right that his father would never have destroyed

his family—including now, his little bird Susanna—in order
to see the hidden face of God? Would I blind myself if Bach
had done so, if Handel had followed suit, if he had sought out
the Chevalier in Tunbridge Wells, as Bach had perhaps or
perhaps not recommended? Or would I hold on to my health
till the last possible breath and last possible note and last possible earthly kiss from my earthly Constanze?

Did what God thought matter that much?

Had he ever listened to me? Was he listening to anyone?

Would anything I wrote, any prayer of music I composed, change his mind, his heart, his plans?

When what mattered, in the long run, was something
else.

What Susanna had retained, what Abel had retained,
what Handel had retained, what Christel would have retained if he were by my side in the city of his birth, what
Jack Taylor would have discovered if he had come to Leipzig
to find Susanna, what we all needed to retain were the last
words of Johann Sebastian Bach.

Everything is song.

Nothing else really mattered.

And that was almost the end of it.

She asked if I did not want to visit her in her room or
if perhaps I was inclined for her to visit my bed at the inn.

And I said no, that my Constanze was waiting for me in
Vienna, that the few nights left to me on this earth were for

my love, for the woman I had imagined asking me to cover her in the cool grass and under the swaying trees amid the laughing flowers.

Susanna understood, she said that she would have responded something similar if her Albrecht were still alive.

We closed the concert hall and, breathing into our bodies the scent of spring so lithesome in the air, walked in silence through the city, so quietly that people who were sleeping might have heard the beating of our two hearts under their dreams, the hearts our mothers had first heard all those years ago in our twin cities, her city and my city, her mother and my mother, her *cor* and my *cor*, our two joyful hearts.

Perhaps that was the only celestial sound and rhythm that could come from her body anymore. Perhaps I had to be content with that, joyful that her heart was so large, that Sebastian's daughter had survived to keep me company, if only for these scant hours. Perhaps that was why I had ultimately come to Leipzig, stayed in Leipzig when I was expected elsewhere, gone to that cemetery at every conceivable hour, not to unearth some mystery that was buried with all those dead men, not to help myself figure out how to die well, but to help, if I could, this lost daughter, this lost sister, this woman whose name no one would remember when they write the history of our time and the halls of the future are overflowing with my music.

As we drew near to my lodging, she asked:

"What's that you were singing just now?"

"Just now? Singing, me? Not a thing."

She insisted. Yes, I had been singing since we had left the concert hall, to myself, in a low voice, but not so low that she could not hear it.

"A song? What song?"

She looked at me in disbelief. "What sort of game is this? You want to get me to sing it, is that it?"

I shook my head. "You're the one who's playing a game. You liked Susanna's song, the one from *Figaro*, admit it. And you want to hear it one more time. Well, if you like it, you'll have to work for it, open up your throat."

She turned in a huff and strode a few paces away and then sauntered back to me.

"In Italian," she said. "Another song in Italian."

"What were the words?"

She didn't speak Italian, she said.

"One word, any word, one syllable. Just say it."

"*Gioia*," she said, "that's what it sounded like. And—and *cor*."

Can it be? Can it be that song? My favorite song? Could it have crept into me from the past and then out of me unawares, nestling from within my memory and into the nocturnal air? If so—and I still cannot recall having murmured it forth—I mustn't let her know, I must now indeed play the game she accused me of just a few seconds ago.

"Sorry. Doesn't ring a bell. You must be hallucinating, little Bach bird. Too big a dinner. Good night—and thanks for the company, for the stories."

I turned to leave and then turned again when I heard a hum, something is drifting out from her that could be confused with a hum. The hint of a tune, its beginning.

And I recognized it. I knew what it was, the song I must have been singing. Had I grown so distant from it, so distant from the jubilant Mozart who had composed it, that I had not even realized what was flowing from inside me?

I hummed it back to her.

Her voice rose a bit more, still holding herself back, still trying to keep her vow of silence, losing the battle against the music that was demanding that she burst into song.

I slowly spooled out the first four words. *Io senti dal contento*, happiness is what I feel, I half muttered, half sang them to her, I cast that promise of *contento* at her, dared her to lift the curse, and at first only her hum accompanied me and then, and then, and then, something more, a voice nobody had heard in the decades since her father had died, and then, and then, and then she joined in, she was joining in. First like a little bird as the hum turned into a warble, and then her ample throat that had been shuttered these forty years began to soar, nothing little about that voice, a woman, not a bird, the woman her father had never known, I sang the next words so she could follow, *pieno di gioia il cor*, the heart is full of joy, hers and mine, *pieno di gioia il cor*, both of us full-throated now, oh, we had wintered far away, she without leaving Leipzig and I wandering Europe, and now, now, now, it was time to find refuge, a home in this music.

When she was done and I was done, when not even the echo of the song remained except inside us both, her eyes were shining.

"Why?"

That is all I ask her. Many *why*s, like starlings, float through my mind, but she answers—after giving it some thought—she answers the *why* she has sung, *why now?*

"My gift to you." And pecks me a quick kiss on the cheek. "It's what you need. As I couldn't use it for my father when he . . . At least I haven't failed you."

I was suddenly trembling. "Is it because I am going to die? Can you see it in my face? You see that I am going to die?"

"We are all going to die."

"But not alone."

"Not alone. If we are lucky, not alone."

She starts to leave, comes back yet one more time.

"You know, I lied to you," she says. "When you asked me if that was all, if my father had not written anything else to Handel. I lied to you. There was one more thing."

I do not dare to ask her what it is, what other wonder she has for me this evening.

"*Heaven is where everybody sings, whether they have a voice or not.* That was what my father told Handel at the very end of his letter, what Abel told me."

"And why didn't you tell me when I asked you?"

"Because if I had told you, I would have had to— because it wasn't the only lie."

She scurried her hand under her petticoat and extracted a scant roll of yellowed paper, bundled up with an old piece of string. She smoothed the paper out.

I looked at the title.

The *Et Incarnatus Est.*

"I lied," she said again. "I wanted to burn it when they murdered my Albrecht, I wanted to so badly my fingers were on fire. But kept it. Perhaps I guessed that someday someone would come along, as my father suggested, a man like you who could put it to good purpose. It's yours."

"You don't want to sing it now, with me?"

"I lost my chance when my father died. It's yours. Or don't you want it? You prefer that I burn it in front of your eyes."

She looked around and saw a torch nearby on the street, just outside the Gasthof, where the sign of the Three Swans shone in the glimmering dark. I followed her eyes. I followed her eyes and her intention and snatched the paper from her hands.

And read and mouthed and imagined the last music Sebastian Bach had ever composed.

It cradles out from the sheet as if a chorus of angels has settled in my ears, gentling me into a final dream. It was the most serene song that had ever blessed my existence. What I would hope might be intoned at my funeral—or better still, as I died, that someone should whisper this into my ear to ease, as Susanna's father had desired for himself, my way into eternity. The face of God, the face of God. What each of us hopes will rock us to sleep when our moment comes, help us cross that river, so that we do not fear becoming a body that will resurrect and also do not fear dying forever and ever.

I cannot tell how much time is left to me. Or when the sadness will again seize me by the throat, ask me questions no man and no woman can really answer, try to crush me into silence, why me, why me, why must everything I love die along with the world?

Meanwhile, there is this song. A song for Maman in Paris and a song for Papa in Salzburg and a song for Johann Sebastian Bach in Leipzig. A song for those who languish in London cemeteries, Johann Christian Bach and Carl Friedrich Abel, Handel and Jack Taylor and his father. A song for my little dead brothers. A song for my children, who died in Vienna. A song for all the dead and a song for all those who await a similar death, including the forgotten sisters of the world, my sister and Christel's sister and Abel's sister, a song for all the sisters and all the brothers, and for this orphaned brother, this Wolfgang destined to disappear.

May I sing it, Sebastian's song of peace, may I find my own song to accompany it, may I sing something similar when the future grows dark and blind, may I be blessed to smile a little nothing at Death when Death comes for me, when I can keep Death away no more. A Requiem, from the moment we are born we humans are always singing some sort of Requiem for ourselves, and all the other souls, the only sin if that Requiem were not to celebrate joy and life as we fade away. What I half learned that night and morning in London, what I groped to discover during those months in Paris, what this visit to Leipzig has finally taught me thanks to Bach's message and his little messenger, his own flesh and blood.

What more can I ask for? What more can I take back to the light of my love, the love of my light, my Constanze?

Heaven is a place where everybody sings, whether they have a voice or not.

I can only hope, hope and pray, pray and hope, that when the moment comes, as I say good-bye, everything, everything will be song.

SOME MOLTO VIVACE
ACKNOWLEDGMENTS

Like all my work, this one would not be possible without the constant presence of my wife Angélica by my side. She has not only accompanied me during the search for the human, historical, and literary keys of this narrative, but has also been the indispensable reader of each of its multiple versions, as well as interminably and fruitfully listening with me to the panoply of music that pulses through the text.

It is thanks to my brother-in-law, Ryan Dilley, that *Allegro* was born. The impetus to compose it came during a dinner in London with him and Nathalie, Angélica's sister, when we first learned of the existence of the enigmatic Dr. Taylor and his surgical relations with Bach and Handel, leading me to announce, even before dessert was served, that this was a story that needed to be told (though Mozart had not yet visited me to demand that he be the one to tell it).

My assistant and dear friend, Suzan Senerchia, worked hard, with the help of Duke University librarians, on archives and documents to provide references about diseases, medicine, burials, blindness, patronage, and concerts, as well as other events of that time that allowed me to transmit it with some degree of verisimilitude and density. She also kept at bay those who would steal from me the hours I needed to figure out what had happened that night when Johann Sebastian Bach and the Eye Surgeon had their fateful and enigmatic meeting.

I have an enormous debt of gratitude to my agents at Wylie: Jacqueline Ko, Kristi Murray, Jennifer Bernstein, and Thomas Wee. They have never flagged in their support for my books and profuse projects, always enthusiastic and oh so patient. I wish Mozart had, during his persistent struggle for recognition, entertained such loyalty. And as for Raquel de la Concha and Marilu Casquero, my friends and agents in Spain, where *Allegro* was first published in the language of Cervantes, they were the first to recognize the need for this story to find its way into the world.

Regarding (in several senses of the word) my editor, Judith Gurewich, no praise is sufficient to express her importance, my joy (allegro indeed!) that she has become part of my life and Angélica's since we met on the journey that would lead to *The Suicide Museum*. Her crucial observations about the text and how to make it better were both wise and delightful. I treasure her friendship.

She has been, of course, seconded by an admirable group at Other Press: Yvonne Cárdenas, Lauren Shekari, Janice Goldklang, Jessica Geer, Ilisha Stevens, Gage Desser, Alex Poreda, Terrie Akers, and Shawn Nichols (with a nod to Zoë, Mona, Bill, and Ed). I appreciate the creative and careful way in which they have all, in one way or another, sustained the work and helped its publication and reception.

Alas, there are many who cannot read these words and who will never know of my gratitude to them. Bach, Handel, Carl Friedrich Abel, and Johann Christian have enlightened me for decades before they found a voice in this narrative, and as for Mozart, my not-so-secret collaborator, oh, as to Mozart... When I was asked, many years ago, to identify three wishes, one of them was that he could have been granted a few more years of life. I feel that he and the others, with their glorious music, are the coauthors of my novel, reserving as well gratitude for the forgotten women of history, such as Susanna Bach and Mozart's mother, Anna Maria, without whose inspiration from the other side of death I would not have been able to finish this celebration of humanity and love.

My penultimate thanks are for those living members of my family who have, however unknowingly, contributed to this book: Rodrigo, Joaquín, Isabella, Catalina, Deena, Heather, Cecilia, Kayleigh, Emmy, Sharon and Kirby, Ana María and Pedro, Patricio and Marisa. And the friends who are so many that I dare not begin to name them, one by one, lest these acknowledgments turn into yet another novel. But you know who you are.

And Eric, thank you for reading this novel before you died. I am sure that you understood why, along with Angélica, I dedicated this Allegro tribute to everlasting friendship to you.

PLAYLIST COMPANION TO *ALLEGRO*

PRELUDE
Mozart's Church Sonata no. 1 in E-Flat Major
"Et in unum Dominum" from Johann Sebastian Bach's Mass in B
Minor

CHAPTER ONE: LONDON
The first movement, Andante, of Johann Christian Bach's Sinfonia
Concertante in C Major (W. C 36a) for Two Violins and Cello
Solo
And later, the cello solo from the same sinfonia concertante
J. C. Bach's Piano Concerto in D Major, op. 13, no. 2: the second
movement, "con spirito"
The "La Paix" movement from Handel's *Music for the Royal Fireworks*
Mozart's aria "Va, dal furor portata" (first chords)
The march from Mozart's *The Marriage of Figaro*
Second movement from Vivaldi's Mandolin Concerto in C Major
The second movement, Largo, from Vivaldi's Concerto for Two
Oboes, Strings, and Basso Continuo in C Major, RV 534
The "La Paix" movement from Handel's *Music for the Royal Fireworks*

"Total eclipse! / No sun, no moon, / All dark amid the blaze of noon," aria from Handel's *Samson*

The last part of the second movement from Carl Friedrich Abel's Sinfonia Concertante for Violin, Oboe, Clarinet, and Orchestra in B-Flat Major

J. S. Bach's Prelude no. 1 in C Major, from *The Well-Tempered Clavier*, which imitates the harmony of birdsong

Mozart's Piano Sonata no. 11 in A Major: the first two movements, the Andante grazioso and the Menuetto

J. S. Bach's *Art of the Fugue*, Contrapunctus XIV

"Et Incarnatus Est" from J. S. Bach's Mass in B Minor (it will be repeated later)

The Adagio from Mozart's Fantasia for Piano in C Minor, K. 475

CHAPTER TWO: PARIS

All three movements of Mozart's *Paris* Symphony, no. 31

Jean-Baptiste Lully's *Marche pour la cerémonie des Turcs*

First movement from Mozart's Piano Sonata no. 8 in A Minor, K. 310

Mozart's twelve variations on "Ah, vous dirai-je, Maman" ("Twinkle, Twinkle, Little Star")

And again Abel's Sinfonia Concertante in B-Flat Major

The second movement, Largo Presto Largo, from Mozart's music for the ballet *Les Petits Riens*. And then the Larghetto

Mozart's Sonata for Piano and Violin no. 21 in E-Minor

The Benedictus from Bach's Mass in B Minor

And again "La Paix," from *Music for the Royal Fireworks*

Again, Mozart's Piano Sonata no. 8 in A Minor

EPILOGUE: LEIPZIG

Benedictus from Mozart's Mass in C Major, K. 337 "Solemnis"

"Non più andrai," from *The Marriage of Figaro*

Aria from Mozart's *Don Giovanni*: "Vivan le femmine, viva il buon vino! Sostegno e gloria d'umanità!"

The aria "Deh vieni, non tardar," from *The Marriage of Figaro*

The aria "Crystal streams in murmurs flowing," from Handel's oratorio *Susanna*

Tempo di Minuet (WKO188) from Abel's solo music for viola da gamba. If unavailable, the Adagio (WKO189)

Again, Bach's Contrapunctus XIV

"Deeper, and deeper still," an aria sung by a tenor from Handel's oratorio *Jephtha*, followed by the chorus: "How dark, O Lord, are Thy decrees, / All hid from mortal sight"

The duet "Mi sento dal contento," from Mozart's *The Marriage of Figaro*

And again "Et Incarnatus Est" from the Mass in B Minor

And again the Church Sonata no. 1 in E-Flat Major

Mozart's Sinfonia Concertante in E-Flat Major

ABOUT THE AUTHOR

Ariel Dorfman is a Chilean-American author, born in Argentina, whose award-winning books in many genres have been published in more than fifty languages and his plays performed in more than one hundred countries. Among his works are the plays *Death and the Maiden* and *Purgatorio*, the novels *The Suicide Museum* (Other Press, 2023), *Widows*, and *Konfidenz*, and the memoirs *Heading South, Looking North* and *Feeding on Dreams*. He writes regularly for the *New York Times*, *Washington Post*, *Los Angeles Times*, *New York Review of Books*, *The Nation*, *The Guardian*, *El País*, and CNN. His stories have appeared in *The New Yorker*, *The Atlantic*, *Harper's*, *The Threepenny Review*, and *Index on Censorship*, among others. A prominent human rights activist, he worked as press and cultural advisor to Salvador Allende's chief of staff in the final months before the 1973 military coup, and later spent many years in exile. He lives with his wife Angélica in Santiago, Chile, and Durham, North Carolina, where he is the Walter Hines Page Emeritus Professor of Literature at Duke University.